WHAT IF THE EMBER DIDN'T DIE,
BUT STARTED A FIRE?

THE

COMPASSION

FIRE

KATY HOLLWAY

SozoPrint.com

ISBN 978-0-9929404-6-1

Other titles in this series:
The Compassion Prize
The Compassion Gift

Other titles from this author:
The Times of Kerim
The Days of Eliora

For Asher,
You face adversity with courage and humour.
You are an inspiration.

For Stephen,
Your encouragement and enthusiasm have immense impact.
You lead by example and not just by words.

... And for those that protect and nurture the ember,
then breathe life into it until it becomes a fiery beacon.

Chapter 1

The smell of acrid smoke from the crumpled and burning drone drifted in through the window. Its carcass was now engulfed in flames in the manicured garden of Harland Barret. The same Harland Barret that lay dead on the window seat of the library.

There was a confusing mixture of emotion; tears of sadness and grief were flowing alongside wide smiles and laughter.

The Emundabit cube was lifeless. They were safe. Everything was going to change.

Luca had been so relieved when he had seen Mercy and Eban running from the refuse truck across the lawn at the mansion. Brigadier Alard had been with them, carrying the injured body of Harland Barret. Luca's first encounter with the Brigadier and Campion, the people who were free from Tropolis rule, did not rest well with his own changed and awakened heart. Campion had sea forts and land settlements and certainly appeared to go about life idly without caring for those that needed help. Luca wanted freedom for Outside, and for Tropolis to be rid of the fatigue. Both could find their answer in the engagement of Campion.

A cry for help painted on the very walls of Outside had changed everything. It was as if a spark had suddenly been given life and Campion had responded.

Mercy, Eban and Alard had arrived together directly from Outside where they had been working with the Campion team to liberate the people. Before they had come to the mansion Eban had even sent a video message to the Network in Tropolis to tell them that they were coming to help before sending the fleets of boats to the city. True compassion was on its way.

Luca felt he could breathe easily once again or maybe for the first time. His people would be free. There was, at last, a reason for them to fight for life and not just existence. He coughed on the bitter taste that hung in the air.

Harland wasn't supposed to be dead. He wasn't even supposed to still be at the mansion. Mara Hutchings who had been ruling under the guise of Harland had come to collect him to ensure that her power was not challenged in the aftermath of Emundabit. She would have, of course, let Harland take any damaging blame from those that were safe in the ark if they had ever decided to think for themselves. But she had not been carried in with Harland and the drone she had planned to escape in, still emitted vast plumes of black smoke as it burned in the garden.

Brigadier Alard had sat and wept with Kelsee as Harland Barret died. Luca had asked why Alard would fight so hard for the life of Harland only to be told that a fair trial would be what all the people, Tropolites, Campion and Outsiders, would call for. If he had survived, it would have been easier for all the people to understand the way things had been run in Tropolis for the past years. Luca had wanted him to live too.

'Brigadier Alard! Come in Alard!'

The lingering moment of sweet success was broken.

Alard tapped his shoulder and spoke into the communicator. 'Alard receiving. Go ahead Thomas.'

'Request your presence at the entrance to Tropolis, sir,' Major Thomas began, her voice layered with the muffled sounds of shouting and loud bangs. 'Resistance from the city is violent.'

'On our way! Over and out.' Alard brushed down his uniform and straightened his shoulders. 'Let's go!' he said, beckoning them all to follow.

'Why are they resisting?' Eban asked. 'We sent the Outsiders and Campion in to help.'

Luca gasped. 'A message went out over the Network.' He caught Kelsee's gaze. 'They think we are attacking them. The video you sent didn't make it in one piece. Hutchings mashed it about and broadcast it telling the Tropolites to protect the city.'

'That's not what I said at all!' Eban exclaimed. 'I told them we were coming and bringing the cure for their compassion fatigue. That we wanted to extend a hand of friendship not conflict.'

'That's not what we heard,' Kelsee said, wiping her face on her sleeve. She winced as one of the paper strips holding the cut on her cheek closed caught on the fabric.

'Let's go!' Alard said impatiently.

'What about my grandfather?' Kelsee said, her voice shaking a little. 'We need to bury him.'

'There is no time. My people need assistance.' Alard replied clinically.

'We can't just leave him here!'

Mercy took the throw from the chair and covered Harland's body. 'There is little more that we can do here.' She grasped Kelsee's shoulder. 'Your people need assistance too and they need it now.'

Kelsee stifled a sob and looked up at Alard. 'We could use my grandfather's Maglev carriage.' She bent low and gathered up the papers that she and Luca had removed from the safe. 'We should take these,' she said glancing up at Luca.

'No time,' Alard stated firmly from the doorway.

Mercy frowned at Alard. 'Here!' she said, passing Kelsee a neat leather document bag.

'You're right.' Luca crouched and stacked a few more papers and handed them to Kelsee. 'If Harland had locked them away, there is bound to be something of value in them.'

'It might be what we need to convince the world that he wasn't completely to blame,' Kelsee said hopefully.

Luca took a deep breath but did not reply. Harland Barret may not have been ruling at the very end, but he had been the one that had instigated the building of Outside and the mistreatment of the ones it contained. But in the only conversation Luca had ever had with Barret, Luca had offered Harland peace and had gifted him with compassion.

Luca stood. He picked up the tiny cube that had held so much destruction and held it in the palm of his hand. 'He was a clever man,' he began. He recalled the clue that Harland had given them to not only find the cube but to access the termination code. He dropped the dull weapon into his pocket. 'I expect there is evidence that will set the record straight.' He was relieved that these weren't just words to soften Kelsee's grief, but sentiments that he held with conviction. Luca wanted to see fair justice for all parties.

As soon as they left the house Luca understood his unease from before.

'The Maglev is gone!' he shouted.

'Get in the truck!' Alard ordered.

The group dashed around Luca who stood staring at the empty space where the carriage should have been. 'Hutchings!' he whispered.

Kelsee grabbed his sleeve and urged him to follow.

The engine was already humming when Luca climbed inside the cab. It was uncomfortably full, but he squeezed into the space.

'Hutchings has taken the Maglev. She's not dead, she's still out there. That's why the countdown for full Emundabit had been switched on. That's why the Campion sites had been attacked.'

Alard paid no attention to the pathways of the garden. He drove over the miniature hedges and wove through the flower beds.

'Who is this Hutchings person?' he asked.

'Mara Hutchings. She's the one who has been running Tropolis,' Kelsee spoke out clearly. 'It hasn't been my grandfather in charge for years. She's the one you saw trying to escape in the drone; the one that exploded. She's meant to be dead. I thought you killed her.'

Luca looked at Kelsee. Her eyes were puffy from the tears of grief, but her cheeks were flushed with anger.

'The drone was hit and crashed before it had really got into the air. The explosion came moments later, but she could have escaped. Where would she be going?' Alard asked, keeping his attention on his path.

'Could?' Kelsee replied almost spitting out the word. 'She did escape.'

'The ark,' Luca said reaching over to Kelsee and placing his hand over her balled fists. 'If she had started the countdown, that is where she will be heading.' Luca turned to Eban. 'Do you think she will know that the Emundabit countdown has been stopped?'

Eban shrugged. 'She must have started it with something that she had with her.'

'The cube from the holding room that Alec and I rescued you from!' Luca exclaimed as he nodded to Kelsee. She narrowed her eyes and nodded back.

'Hutchings might know what I've done if she looks at it,' Eban said scratching his chin. 'But why would she think I had?' Eban smiled as he looked at Kelsee and then at Luca. 'There's not much I can do about it anyway.'

Kelsee brushed away a tear from her cheek. 'He tried to do his best for me,' she said quietly to Luca. 'He took care of me and made sure I had all I wanted, or at least all he thought I wanted.'

Luca sighed. He wished he knew what to say to comfort her, but he had no words. He gently rubbed her hands until they relaxed a little.

'He didn't know what I needed at all,' Kelsee said sadly. 'He sent me away and I hardly saw him.'

Luca shook his head. 'You don't know that he even did that.'

She stared at Luca.

'We don't know where he finished and Hutchings began.'

Alard roughly followed the route that the truck had taken in the first place, but as soon as they had left the grounds, he seemed to instinctively know which direction to head. Luca understood that Alard had vast knowledge of the landscape, but his direct and assured driving was so confident that Luca wondered how he could navigate the land so well.

The vehicle jumped and jolted over the terrain until it reached a wide but empty road.

Luca tried to take his mind from Alard's understanding and turned to Eban who was sitting furthest away. 'Is there any way to get your message out again?' he asked. 'The complete message?'

'I can't do anything from here,' Eban answered. 'I sent it out live via a security camera on site in Outside, hacked into the Network and everything.'

'They have a copy of the whole thing in Tropolis, in the media suite.' Luca turned to Alard. 'If you can get us to the main entrance building where the Compassion Prize contestants enter, I think we can get that message broadcast properly. Maybe if they see the whole thing, the Tropolites will know that they don't need to fight and let Major Thomas and the people in.'

Alard tapped his shoulder, 'Thomas! Don't advance on Tropolis. They think we are going to attack. Over.'

'Received, sir! Drawing the Outsiders and Campion away. Over,' Thomas replied, the noise of the crowd muffling her voice a little.

'Retreat using the fleet as a buffer. Await further orders. Over.'

'Agreed. Will keep contact open. Over.'

Alard turned to Luca. 'We can take the rubbish chute into the city.'

Luca half laughed. He thought of his notebook with the gentle Campion flower painted on the front. It felt like a lifetime ago that he had gleaned it from the heaps of Outside. The pages had recorded the escape path, the rubbish hatch and the details of so many that had left Tropolis and the Death Room. Freedom had been with the rubbish. Luca knew the route because he had used it before.

Mercy shook her head. 'The place where the barges are loaded is next to the jetty with all the expensive boats. There is too much security, especially as Major Thomas and the others are coming by boat. I'm not sure that will work with the Tropolite people already on high alert.'

'I think there is another way in,' Alard said slowly. 'There is a direct Maglev line from the Endurance test site to the contestants' building. I think this truck could take out the fence further along the line and closer to the tunnel. We know the weak spots. My jeep could probably take us the rest of the way.' He accelerated and tapped his shoulder once again. 'Thomas!'

'Yes, sir!'

'Get in contact with Ground level three. Captain Scout has my jeep. Tell her to bring it and a crew of as many as she can muster to meet on the outskirts before tunnel 16. Over.'

'Message received. I'll contact you when ground level three confirm the jeep and crew are nearing tunnel 16. Over and out.'

Alard drove with more determination than before. The road stretched out ahead of them, straight and clear from obstruction.

The illustration of the rare Campion flower could not have been further from the truth when it came to the organisation. Sweet and delicate colours were not what marked this group at all. Even Mercy's harsher version of the flower tattooed on her neck didn't seem to capture the passion that had been awakened in Alard. Luca recalled the hurried and dripping call for help painted on the wall of Outside. This was perhaps the closest representation to Campion that Luca could make; red for passion, not perfect in form, but bold. Campion had been hidden away and may have even been on the brink of extinction, but this little movement was not dead yet. They had come alive at last, and they must now fight to be seen.

'Don't you think that the people who own the boats will be in the ark?' Kelsee asked turning to Luca and shaking him from his thoughts.

'Only if the ark is still in use.' Luca replied quietly.

'What are you talking about?' Mercy questioned. 'What is this ark?'

Luca blew out a breath. 'Hutchings arranged for a safe place to run while everyone else died. It is huge and under the buildings where they took us for the Compassion Prize. They wouldn't need to come out for years if they didn't want to. I have no idea who would go there or who would be invited.'

'Would they be there now?'

Luca thought for a moment. If there was no way of telling that Emundabit had been stopped there would be no reason for the chosen few to not be in the ark. 'I think they are,' he eventually said.

They travelled in silence for a long while. Luca couldn't help but think of his mother and the drones that had been sent to her settlement. Had they been recalled in time or had they started their work? He wondered if she had been evacuated with the rest or had stayed as stubbornly as before. He hoped that someone had been able to convince her.

Alard eventually took the truck off the smooth road. The smaller track was rough and uncomfortable. Being tightly packed into the cab only meant that they were even more likely to bash heads.

Thankfully, after driving around the rim of a lake and emerging through a bank of trees the truck came to a standstill at the chain-link fence beside a Maglev line.

'Just a little further,' Alard said. 'This is not going to be easy.'

He drove as gently as he could alongside the fence, but the ground was uneven and there was no road to follow.

Luca felt bruised and achy by the time Alard eventually stopped the truck. Sitting a little distance away was the familiar jeep, Captain Debs Scout and a few older men and a little further still tunnel 16, the entrance to Tropolis.

Alard climbed out of the rubbish truck. 'Where is everyone?' he asked.

Scout still wore her slightly faded blue jacket, it stood out against the earthy tones. She leaned in and spoke softly to Alard. Luca could not make out what was discussed in hushed tones.

'How did she get here?' Luca asked knowing that her role was with the sea forts.

'Scout went with me into Outside,' Eban replied. 'Alard bought her with him when we came after you. She was dropped off on an errand near Campion.'

Alard turned to the friends. 'Everyone in the jeep. Let's go!'

Luca saw that Alard was pale.

Eban unlocked the section at the edge of the flatbed end to the jeep, climbed up and then offered help to Mercy, but she had already clambered up. Luca lifted Kelsee to the edge and climbed up after her. They sat a little huddled together. In the back of the jeep was the boat that they had used to cross the cavern lake. There was a wide enough gap between the craft and the sides of the flatbed to sit in. They were joined by two of the Campion crew. Alard swapped places with Captain Scout and clambered into the front seat of the jeep.

Luca squeezed Kelsee's hand and winked at her. She smiled faintly. He then turned to watch through the back window and front windscreen.

Scout revved the rubbish truck engine and accelerated at the fence. It could not resist the force but put up a fight by springing back when the truck reversed. After a few attempts the steel posts bent low and the fence gave up but would not lay flat. The truck pulled forward further so that the jeep could manoeuvre towards the tunnel; the front bumper of the truck was almost touching the Maglev rail.

Alard carefully edged the jeep towards the gaping mouth.

But the tunnel was no longer dark. A single spot of light was growing stronger and brighter and larger.

Scout shouted as she jumped out of the cab.

Alard threw the jeep into reverse.

A Maglev was advancing on them at high speed.

Chapter 2

The fence jolted as the jeep reversed over it and out into the sparse undergrowth. The vehicle spun about.

Luca grabbed at the side of the flatbed to keep himself steady. He gasped as the Maglev rushed from the deep gloom.

There was a moment when it felt like time had slowed down even though the Maglev still raced on. Luca noticed the smashed section in the window at the front of the first carriage and watched as car after car exited the tunnel. He glanced at the rubbish truck, abandoned, next to the rail and covered his ears.

A thundering bang reverberated in the clearing as the Maglev collided with the truck. The heavy vehicle was pushed along the track a short distance twisting slightly as it went, far enough that the fence was released from its front wheels. Gravel and dust spat into the air in a dark cloud. The screech of tearing metal made Luca wince. The back of the truck caught on a thicker steel post that had been set into concrete where a join in the chain link occurred. It jammed in place between the post and the front of the Maglev.

The front of the train came to a sudden stop. The back of the first carriage lifted from the rail taking the second car with a deafening and sustained moan. One by one the carriages concertinaed behind the first, scraping and grinding as the walls buckled and split and the glass shattered. The crumpled mess blocked the tunnel.

Luca stood as the jeep halted. His shoulders drooped. 'No!' he whispered.

Luca glared at the rubbish truck. If only it had been moved away from the rail, then the entry into the tunnel would still be free. The front end had been completely smashed; the cab was crushed under the weight of the speeding train. Dark smoke began to rise from the engine as sparks flashed. A dark liquid ran from the underside and was pooling beneath the vehicle.

Scout lifted herself from the bracken and leaves and brushed the muck from her trousers. She turned from the wreckage and started to jog towards the jeep.

A series of sharp bangs punctuated the silence. Scout fell to the ground.

The two Campion men that were in the jeep pulled out small hand guns and ducked behind the rim of the flatbed.

'Get down!' Alard shouted and accelerated towards Scout. He pulled the jeep around the front of her, flung open the door and jumped out.

A couple more shots rang out. Everyone dipped. One of the Campion men motioned for the friends to get away from the covered boat. Luca struggled to stay low but as soon as they had moved clear the Campion guard lifted the boat to provide some cover.

Alard grabbed Scout and lifted her, holding her at her waist. She cradled one arm close to her body.

Luca cautiously peered through the window.

Scout was injured but not badly enough that she couldn't move. Alard pushed her into the jeep and she slid along the seat, ducking below the glass.

A bullet hit the side window and it shattered spraying diamond shards across the seat and Scout's back.

Alard climbed into the jeep.

Luca dared to look again. He saw several men dressed in fluorescent waterproofs clambering out from the broken carriages. The Campion crew in the jeep opened fire at them. One man collapsed and lay unnaturally twisted in the remains of the Maglev. Another two ducked into the voids of the train.

Luca was familiar with the outfits; the Tropolite workers wore them at the docks when the weather was foul or cold while the Outsiders had to endure the elements as they gleaned. What were they doing here? They were dazed, and bloody cuts marred their faces and hands.

Luca shook his head and frowned. 'Stop!' he called and raised his hand. These men didn't carry guns and did not appear to be the threat.

He scanned the disfigured Maglev. In a surviving carriage that seemed to perch high above the others, resting on the broken shards, there were two more people. They wore the uniform of the Tropolis army and pointed their weapons at the jeep. Luca gasped when he recognised the vindictive smile of his enemy in Tropolis.

A waft of blackened smoke blew between the two parties and his face was hidden. There was a sudden bang as large orange flames rose from the truck wreckage. A ball of putrid gases, smoke and fire mushroomed from the engine followed by a second and deeper explosion.

Luca shielded Kelsee as he had done before, but she did not look away this time.

Alard accelerated from the scene using the smoke as a screen, the jeep jumping and jolting as it went. The Campion guards didn't put their guns away.

'Thickset and Atticus!' Luca hissed.

Mercy peered back. 'How?' she said, 'They were taken and locked in the staff quarters shipping container in Outside.'

Eban peered through the window at Captain Scout and frowned. 'We need to think about why not how.'

'I don't understand,' Luca replied.

Kelsee nodded. 'Why weren't they heading for Tropolis?' She looked hard at Luca.

'You're right,' Luca said. 'That Maglev was the one that Alec took Kelsee to Tropolis in. They must have summoned it to Outside to pick them up. But it was heading away from Tropolis not to it. We needed to go through that tunnel to get into the city, but they were coming out of it.' Luca gritted his teeth. 'And now they've blocked it.'

Eban banged on the window. Alard twitched a quick look back at him. 'We need to stop!' Eban shouted. He pointed at Scout. 'Debs' wound needs treating!'

Alard nodded but kept driving.

'Speaking about people not being where they should be,' Luca said. 'What is Captain Scout doing here? Shouldn't she be with the rest of the Campion force?'

Eban turned and sat down once again. He lifted his feet as the boat was laid flat once again. 'She went with me and a small group into Outside to help with the evacuation,' he said explaining to Luca and Kelsee. 'Alard was going to leave her with the boats and Outsiders, just like you said, but then he thought that it would be best to bring a member of staff back to his post since no one else knows how to operate the radio. It would help with the communication, for them know when to bring the others into Tropolis.'

'Well, I guess she could have helped at the tunnel,' Luca replied staring at his dirty hands.

Mercy was quick to answer. 'She did help at the tunnel.'

Luca didn't look up. He heard the reprimand in Mercy's voice.

He knew Mercy would step in to guard Scout again if he said anything further, but he couldn't help thinking that Scout's mistake might have cost them many lives. He tried to think of those that were waiting at the violent edge of Tropolis as well as those that were sick. He tried and failed. He was not feeling anxious, he was angry. He shook his head a little as he tried to shake it off. He looked out into the stumpy trees and scrubland.

He wanted to get to Tropolis and set the Network broadcast right. He wanted to stop Hutchings.

'Do you think Hutchings needed that tunnel?' Luca asked.

Eban shrugged.

Luca turned to the Campion men. 'Is that the route the Maglev would take from Barret's mansion?'

'What mansion?' the men questioned.

'Never mind!' Luca said sullenly.

The vehicle stopped. Eban jumped from the flatbed and climbed into the cab. Luca could see him opening up the blood-soaked sleeve. Alard stepped out of the cab.

'Will she be alright?' Mercy asked.

'The bullet only made a superficial injury,' he informed them.

'The Maglev ...'

'Luca!' Mercy said a frown.

'He said superficial. I'm glad that she will be alright but there are things that we are trying to do.' Luca could hear his own smarting tone. Mercy may not have deserved it, but he would not take it back. He turned to Alard. 'The Maglev from the mansion, would it have to go through that tunnel back there?'

'Yes, but it probably went through already.'

'Maybe, but surely that would have meant a crash inside or at the other end.'

'True!' Alard said with a questioning tone.

'And that Maglev came from Outside,' Luca began.

'From Outside?' Alard said nodding. 'That tunnel is shorter than the one to Outside, but does connect with it. If that Maglev was in the tunnel first, Harland's Maglev would have to wait at the passing point further up the track. You can't bypass it with a code because it is to stop collisions with other Maglev cars.' He looked intently at the path he had taken. 'I shouldn't have left.'

'Yes, you should,' Mercy replied. 'We were under attack.'

Alard began to get agitated. 'But if Hutchings was heading that way, we could have stopped her.'

'Let's go back!' Luca suggested.

Alard looked at Luca and then at the girls. 'I can't put you in more danger than necessary.'

Eban called from the cab. 'I've patched her up!'

Alard leaned in. 'Are you able to walk Debs?'

'It's my arm, sir, not my legs!'

'So, you should be fine taking the kids back to ground level three from here?' Alard opened the back of the jeep and ushered them forward. 'You three and Eban are going with Captain Scout back to the Campion land settlement.' He beckoned them to move faster. 'I'm going with the rest to see if I can get to Hutchings.'

'I want to come!' Luca said.

Kelsee stepped forward clutching the leather case of files. 'Me too!' she demanded angrily.

Alard looked directly at Kelsee. 'I'm not taking you.' He glanced at Luca. 'Either of you.'

Eban and Scout got out of the jeep as Alard climbed back in.

Luca could feel the burn in his cheeks as Alard pulled away. 'I'm not a kid!' he shouted. The words made no difference to either Alard or to Luca's anger.

Eban walked up to Luca. 'And that isn't a tantrum?' he said patting Luca on the back. Luca turned ready to fight but was caught off guard by Eban's cheery grin. 'Mate! Let someone else fight for a bit. I don't want you to get shot.' He leaned in close and whispered. 'Come on, if Scout was able to be reached by radio and was waiting for the command to take everyone into Tropolis she must have access to Alard's comms gear. Think about it, maybe we won't have to go to Tropolis at all.'

Eban had said the right thing. A little bit of hope was able to quench the heat of Luca's rage.

'Which way?' Luca asked Scout. Her arm was held in a makeshift sling made from a belt.

'We'll follow the route the Brigadier was taking.' She began to walk briskly. 'Keep up!'

By the time the friends had traipsed through the mud and reached the side of the road they were tired.

Luca thought that he recognised the pot holed track with plants growing down its middle but perhaps all the Campion roads were made to look like this.

'Not far now,' Scout said pointing with her uninjured arm. 'Oh!'

Luca looked in the direction she indicated. There was dirty grey smoke rising into the sky ahead.

Chapter 3

All signs of weariness fell away as Luca rushed towards the flames.

'Emundabit!' he yelled towards Eban. 'Those codes and commands! Hutchings has set the village alight.'

Luca knew that Eban would have told him not to exaggerate had it not been for the orange glow that was filtering through the trees.

As Luca caught his first glimpse of the houses he noticed that the fire had broken out in several places. There were a couple of buildings at the very edge of the village alight. The flames leapt out of the once boarded windows, but the outer streets were deserted. The real blaze was much further in.

Luca rushed deeper into the settlement. The Campion people that had been left behind had already set up a string of volunteers with buckets. They also had large hoses that spouted copious amounts of water trained on the buildings. It all appeared far too little as the flames reared against the defence. But that would not stop the community.

The people worked harmoniously, obeying the barked orders from an older man dressed in a blue uniform. They were struggling to hold back the fire from the library.

'My mother!' Luca choked out.

He ran to the man who was dressed in Campion uniform assuming he was in charge.

'Don't just stand there!' the man shouted at Luca and the others that were behind him. 'Everyone grab a bucket. Douse the buildings.'

'Is Willow out of there?' Luca asked gripping the man's arm.

'She won't leave the blasted building.' He looked away from the flames for a moment. 'Scout! Is that you?' he yelled out over the roaring of the generator running the pumps and the crackle of the fire. He glanced at Scout's injured arm.

'Grab a radio! I want reports on the farm buildings.'

Scout tapped her shoulder.

'That won't work here,' the man said scowling. 'All those with that rank had been called to Outside. You need a radio.' He flashed the device in his hand at her. 'Go get one from the comms room. We're all on channel six. Go!'

Without hesitation Scout jumped over the hoses and wove through the volunteers.

'Follow her,' Luca screamed.

He didn't check to see if anyone had gone because he had run to the library doors.

Luca coughed on the smoke that was slowly filling up the large room. There were disorganised rows and flipped over chairs as if someone had left in a hurry.

'Willow!' Luca called out.

'Willow!' came Kelsee's echo.

'Get out of here!' Luca ordered angrily as he turned and saw that Kelsee had followed after him.

'Do you think you'll be able to move by yourself?' Kelsee asked.

Luca felt the urgency even more with Kelsee in danger too. 'Willow?' he called again. He frowned and then shouted once again. 'Mother? Where are you?'

'Willow?' Kelsee called, 'We've come to get you out.'

'You won't get me out at all.'

Willow sat in her story chair at the far side of the room. Luca looked about for her wheelchair. It lay on its side some distance away as if it had been pushed out of reach.

'You can't stay here. The fire is coming,' Kelsee said loudly.

Willow covered her mouth as she coughed a little. 'I'm not leaving.'

Luca pushed his way through the rows and stopped just short of his mother. 'You have to leave.'

'There is nothing out there for me,' Willow said shaking her head and lowering her gaze.

'That is ridiculous!' Kelsee replied, pushing the wheelchair closer. 'Now get in.' Willow closed her eyes and turned away for Kelsee.

Luca scowled at his mother. 'This is not the time to hate her! She's with me and we are trying to stop you from burning alive!' Luca pulled on his mother's arm. 'Get in!'

'Don't make us force you,' Kelsee said.

Willow opened her eyes to glare at Kelsee. 'Oh, we wouldn't want anyone to think that a Barret would force anyone to do anything, would we?' Willow hissed. 'It's not in a Barret's nature to do such a thing is it?' She pressed her hand over Luca's urgent pulls. 'Why is she still with you? Get rid of her!' She gripped a battered book in one hand and gripped the chair with the other. 'She can't speak to me like that.'

'I'll speak to you whatever way I like!'

'Show some respect,' Willow demanded. 'I'm his mother.'

Kelsee's cheeks burned. 'What's being a mother got to do with it?' Kelsee asked screwing up her nose. 'I've never had a mother, so I wouldn't know how to talk to them. Get in the chair.'

'Enough!' Luca shouted. 'Kelsee is trying to save you. So am I.'

'I don't want to be saved,' Willow said shaking her head. 'I am better here, with my books.'

'You can't exist in these false worlds,' Luca said prying her hand from the arm of the chair. 'You have to look up and live in this world.' He turned to Kelsee, but she had already moved towards Willow.

'Leave me alone!' Willow protested as they pulled her from the story chair.

'I'm not going to do that!' puffed Luca.

The deep creak vibrated through the building and a large crack began to form across the ceiling above them.

Luca looked up, his heart racing. He fought the urge to hide.

The smoke was thickening, and Luca's eyes were stinging. Breathing was becoming difficult.

'Please mum, help us!' he begged, coughing.

Willow stopped resisting. 'Please don't take me out there. I don't want to face it.' She began to cough violently and retched.

Luca lifted her and twisted her so that she could sit in the wheelchair. 'I'm not leaving you here. I can't do that again.'

Kelsee pushed the chairs aside creating a wider aisle for Luca to push his mother through.

Suddenly, the ceiling over the far corner of the room collapsed with a crash, billowing smoke and dust. Burning roof beams fell to the floor. Luca and Kelsee rushed for the door.

The air outside the library was hot, but clearer. They ran to the other side of the street as the dust spilled out after them.

Water was being sprayed high onto the roof top, but Luca knew that this building could not be saved. He tried to not hear his mother's weeping over the books that would be lost, but it was no use.

'Please,' she begged, 'take me anywhere but here.'

'Nowhere is safe, Willow,' Kelsee replied. 'The whole town has been attacked.'

Willow turned in her chair to glare at Kelsee. 'And whose fault is that?'

'Enough!' Luca yelled. 'You have no right to accuse her!'

'I don't know what type of poison she has fed you, but you are not the Luca I know.'

Luca shook his head. 'I'll never be the Luca that you think you know. I've been orphaned for too long.' He could taste the bitterness of his words and he looked away as his eyes filled with tears.

Eban rushed towards them and threw his arms around Luca. The tension and fear melted away. His mother may have left him, and his father may have hidden, but Luca was no longer without family.

'Mercy went after Debs, but she didn't want you left alone.' Eban pulled away and looked into Luca's face. 'Are you alright?'

'I will be.'

Eban nodded and placed his hand on Luca's shoulder. 'I know.' He looked down at Willow, covered in dust and smoke streaked skin and clothes 'Nice to see you again!' He smiled at her. 'I expect you were glad to see Luca.'

Willow frowned.

Eban smiled. He turned to Kelsee. 'Mercy and Debs went this way.' Eban began to move away.

'You can't leave my books to burn!' Willow shouted. 'Grab a bucket, get another hose over here.'

'There is more at stake here than your books.' Kelsee said angrily. 'Luca is too kind to say it as it really is, but you, woman, are far too self-centred to notice anything else going on.'

'How dare ...'

'How dare I?' Kelsee said clenching her fists. 'How dare I? Don't you see the rest of your beautiful community burning? What about them? Stop thinking about yourself for once.' Kelsee pulled Luca's arm. 'Leave her here. Let's get the message sent.'

Luca kept hold of the wheelchair for a moment. His mother was shocked but safely away from the burning building, there was little he could do if he stayed with her. He had walked away from her before and knew that he had to do it again.

'Luca! You can't let her talk to me like that,' Willow protested. Luca let go of the chair and turned away. 'Where are you going? Come back! You can't just leave me here!'

Luca turned. 'Are you okay?'

Willow coughed and reached up to touch Luca. 'I am now that you are here.'

Luca shook his head and stepped away. 'I'm not staying with you.'

'But you came and rescued me,' Willow recounted. 'You found me. You can find me somewhere safe.'

Luca bit down on his lip. 'You've been somewhere safe this whole time and never thought about anyone but yourself. You put yourself in danger.'

'I was looking after my books.'

'No! You were being stubborn and selfish.' Luca pointed to the burning building. 'You would have died in there.' He glanced at Kelsee then back at Willow. 'We nearly all died in there.' He could feel himself shaking and then a small and steady hand clasped his. Kelsee knew that he needed her to rescue him.

'Don't choose her!' Willow demanded. 'She's a Barret.'

'Not all of us behave like our family.' Kelsee said. 'You should be proud of your son.'

Luca looked at his mother. She showed no sign of even hearing what Kelsee had said let alone feeling it. 'Do what you can to help them,' he said to her walking away with Kelsee. Luca wasn't sure what Willow could possibly do to help; it appeared that she had only ever helped herself since she had arrived.

Eban jogged on ahead with Kelsee and Luca following closely behind. The streets were full of people helping counteract the attack on their village. The fires burned in several separate locations. The library seemed to be a major target with three adjacent buildings ablaze. Further up the road there was a more open area with a parade of houses joined together and a quadrangle in the centre. These buildings were also alight and six blue Campion uniformed people were in charge of ensuring this section was attended to. This fire, as it was more isolated from other buildings, seemed to be under more control. There were scorch marks across the street where the drone had attacked another target. The plants and hedges smouldered but the building had got away with only minor damage to the façade. The large windows were smashed, but this also seemed to be a public building of some kind.

Eban had stopped at the crossroads. He shrugged his shoulders.

'Where now?' Kelsee asked.

Luca looked for more flames. Down a very narrow alley he could see the flickering of another fire. He squinted into the gloom. Mercy was running towards them.

'Down there!' Luca shouted and ran towards Mercy.

'Come quickly!' Mercy beckoned.

Luca let go of Kelsee's hand and ran past Mercy knowing that the flames were significant. All the buildings that burned or were burning were important to this community. The places that the people gathered were the targets. Hutchings wanted Campion dead and had known where to go.

He stopped as he reached the small house on the edge of the community. It was not a public building, but it had to be a significant one.

'Is Scout inside?' Luca asked as Mercy came up behind him.

'No! Debs went in the outhouse down the side.'

Luca's heart raced, and he could feel his hands trembling. The drones hadn't quite hit the target this time, but the flames were growing ever closer as they consumed the unprotected dwelling.

Eban and Luca dashed through the gate that hung to the side of the house and into the small patch of the overgrown walled garden. A low flint outbuilding with a corrugated tin roof nestled at the edge of the undergrowth.

They burst through the door.

Scout was sat at the desk surrounded with monitors and scanners with headphones over her ears. The sudden gust of wind through the open door blew her hair and she turned. Tears were running down her cheeks.

'Get out! You are not authorised personnel.'

She quickly returned to the central screen and switched it off, got up from her chair and ushered them out, shutting the door of what was evidently the communications shed in their faces and bolting it behind them.

Luca turned to the house. Dancing flames were being whipped by the wind and the branches of a nearby tree were now alight.

Several crashes and screams came from inside the flint building.

'No!' Debs shouted. 'This can't be it!'

Luca squinted through the tiny window that was to one side. The glass had been covered over with a thick curtain, but a small section of the pane had been broken. Luca reached inside and lifted the fabric a little to one side. Scout was standing looking down at the floor, and on the desk there was a large space where the monitor had been. 'We've got to get her out of there,' he said as he rushed to the locked door and thumped on it. 'We need to save that equipment.'

'Go away!' Scout shouted from inside.

Eban stepped forward. 'Debs!' he said knocking on the door, 'The house is on fire. You're not safe.'

There was no reply.

Eban tried again. 'You need to get out before it is too late.'

'It's already too late,' she replied. 'It's all my fault! It's all my fault!' she cried.

Chapter 4

There was a grinding of metal as the bolt was undone. Slowly the door was inched open. Luca pushed hard and sent Scout tumbling back into the room.

'What have you done?' he shouted as he dashed forward and bent low over the smashed monitor.

Scout sat silently her head bowed. All the anger had been broken and she was defeated.

'You told them!' Luca accused as he marched up to Scout and snatched the headphones from her. 'What are you telling them now? Fires everywhere, Campion beaten, Outside defeated?'

'Luca!' Mercy said, reaching for him.

'No Mercy! Leave it!' Luca pointed at Scout. 'She told them how to attack.'

The buzzing from the headphones and flickering codes on the other screens could not break the tension.

'Debs?' Eban whispered. 'What's happened?'

Scout covered her face with her hands. 'He's right.' She winced at the pain in her arm but that seemed minor compared to what she felt now. 'It's all my fault.' Her whole body trembled as she sobbed.

Luca drew in a slow steady breath and moved away from the traitor.

Scout peered up as the cord from the headphones was pulled from her fingers. 'But I didn't mean to.'

'How could you not mean to?' Luca shook his head. 'You told Tropolis where to attack. You told them where all the important sites were to ruin this place and take them out.'

'It wasn't like that ... but I know I'm to blame.'

'Yes, you are!' Luca replied through clenched teeth as he leaned in.

'Enough!' Mercy interrupted. She put her hand on Luca's chest and pushed him away a little. 'Debs,' Mercy said turning to Scout and offering a hand to stand, 'What has happened?'

'I've checked the messages,' Debs replied struggling to her feet, 'And he would have had all the information.'

'Who?' asked Eban.

'You need to understand something about me. I'm not Campion born.' Debs lowered her hands but also dipped her head. 'My family escaped Tropolis before the fatigue set in. It was a difficult thing for me, I had friends and a life there. I knew it was right to leave and I have never regretted joining Campion as part of the movement. But when I found out that one of my friends was seriously ill I needed to contact him and find out if there was anything I could do, if I could get him out too.'

'So, you told him where to attack,' Luca accused.

Scout looked up suddenly. 'No!' Her eyes were wide, and she did not break the gaze with Luca. He looked away and grunted. 'No, you have to understand, I didn't know I was telling him.'

Debs turned to the monitor on the floor. 'I've checked the messages we sent. I mention the shops in the square in one message. Then later,' she gently kicked the monitor, 'About the library in another one.' She rung her hands. 'I talked about a meeting at the offices off the main street. I even say that I was recruited and joined up from this building as the headquarters for Campion.' She turned to the friends, appearing more fragile than she had ever been in the past. 'I didn't know he would use the things I said to hurt Campion.'

'He's a Tropolite!' Luca snorted.

'And so am I!' Kelsee said staring hard at Luca. 'Not everyone is like Hutchings.'

Luca blew out a breath and folded his arms.

'I didn't mean to put my people in danger,' Debs said quietly.

'Who was the person you messaged?'

'He wasn't important in Tropolis. In fact, he was so unimportant that he couldn't get any help with his illness. He stopped messaging over three years ago. I think he died.'

Mercy reached out to Debs and placed her hand on her shoulder. 'It isn't your fault.' She quickly turned to Luca who had snorted. 'It isn't!'

Eban bent over the desk. 'These messages you sent, were they secure?'

Debs shrugged. 'There was no need.'

'There obviously was need!' Luca commented.

Mercy turned to him. 'But that is not needed. What has got into you? Stop it! Debs is on our side, don't forget that.'

Eban looked at Debs. 'Messages can be accessed by anyone with a little bit of knowhow.'

'It doesn't matter now. Campion were attacked. There won't be anything left by tomorrow.' Debs sighed and wiped the wetness from her cheeks.

Kelsee gasped. 'Oh!'

'What?' Luca said quickly turning to the open door.

'It's just that if these messages were three years old ...'

Debs interjected. 'Some are even older than that.'

'Yes, well if they are that old, Tropolis may not have all the current information.'

'Did you tell them ...' Luca saw Mercy's frown and corrected himself, 'I mean, did you tell him, about the indoor farms or generators?'

'What farms and generators? No, I was put on duty at the sea forts and haven't been back here for years until Brigadier Alard sent me here today.'

Luca smiled a little and he could feel the squeezing tension lift from his body. 'So those things could still be safe then.' Luca bit down on his lip.

'Campion have food and electricity. It is not lost for them.' Eban smiled. 'Now, who were you on the radio to?'

'My brother. He is manning the sea forts. I was ascertaining what the situation was for the Campion boats and Outsiders. They are still being held back from Tropolis but have found a location to land. It was either that or go back to Outside.' Debs didn't think to stop reporting. 'The towers know that ground level three is in flames.'

'The forts are still standing?' Kelsee asked remembering the Emundabit attack numbers.

'Two towers are down,' Debs said. 'But the drones obviously had the wrong co-ordinates because four towers still stand. Thankfully my brother is in one of them.'

Luca looked at the array of screens fixed to the walls, the computers and gadgets connected to wires. He thought that there must be something that they could use to access the Network and Eban's video from Outside. Suddenly all the buzzing fell silent and the flickering went blank. The power was cut.

Luca leaned out of the door and saw that the flames now licked at the windows and were leaping from the roof of the house.

'We've got to get this stuff out of here!' Luca turned to Eban. 'What do we need?'

'Take as much as you can carry. We'll need the leads too.'

Debs paused momentarily but then bent low and began to unplug everything that she could reach. Kelsee tugged on the curtain at the window which fell away easily. She laid the fabric down, placed the folder of documents from her Grandfather's house in the middle and then began to toss as many items as she could reach on top of it. Mercy pulled leads through the holes in the desk and freed the remaining monitors that were free standing. Eban had opened several drawers and was carefully selecting some items and discarding others.

Kelsee was first to the door. She had gathered up the fabric and carried as much equipment as the curtain would allow. She screamed.

'Get out!' she yelled.

A deep and hollow creaking noise ripped through the crackling flames.

Luca grabbed the pile of things he had manged to gather and rushed for the door. The others were close behind.

The heat was intense as they ran after Kelsee. The large tree that had grown so close to the house was ablaze. The flames dripped down from the dead leaves and spindly branches onto the undergrowth and now the garden was rippling with a dozen smaller fires.

A second creak and a sudden jerk from one of the heavier branches urged the friends to move faster. The dead wood came tumbling down, crashing to the ground in an array of flames, sparks and floating debris that glowed orange.

The friends sped towards the gate that was now flickering. Debs ran ahead gathering all that she had into one hand or balancing it into the others laden arms. She prised it open and held it back. She refused to go through until everyone else had escaped.

Kelsee led the group a safe distance away from the flames. She lowered the bag and let it slump to the pavement. She threw her arms around Luca who almost dropped the things he was carrying.

'I'm so glad we're safe,' she whispered. 'I'm sorry I was angry at you.'

Luca smiled a little and lowered the screen and leads he had to the ground. 'You had every right to be.' He sighed. 'I took it out on Debs when it was Willow I wanted to shout at.'

Kelsee gave a forgiving smile. 'I know what you mean.'

Scout was rummaging through the items caught in the curtain. She picked out a rectangular, palm sized radio. Twisting the dials at the top, she clicked the radio to channel six. A fuzzy voice sounded out.

'I'm sending ten more down to the Library and town hall. The square is now under control. Over.'

'Great. We need as much help as we can get down here. Any news on the farm? Over.'

'Nothing yet. Over.'

Debs raised the radio to her lips and depressed the button. The fuzzy voices disappeared. 'Captain Scout to control, over.'

'Control, receiving. State location and report.'

'I'm in the village, near the comms room. Have managed to gather a radio, but the comms room is destroyed. Fire at the Brigadier's. Over.'

'Damn! Redirect the ten to Alard's place. Over.'

'I hate to say it, sir,' Scout reported, 'But I don't think it would be worth it. The building is too far gone. Over.'

The fuzzy silence was unnerving.

'Alright Captain Scout. Head up to the farm buildings and report back. Over.'

Debs looked up at Eban.

'We'll show you.'

'Message received and understood, sir. Over and out.' She clipped the radio to her belt and sighed. 'Lead the way.'

Luca frowned. 'What about all this?' He gestured towards the heap of leads, screens and other comms equipment. 'We need to set this up somewhere and get that video released.'

Scout turned. 'My priority is my people here. I have been given orders to check on the farm buildings.'

He could feel the heat rising in his cheeks. 'Your priority is not ours.' Luca turned to Eban. 'What can we use of this lot?'

'There is no time for this,' Scout said with force. 'Point me in the direction of the farm buildings.'

Mercy took a deep breath. Luca noticed her pale complexion and how her shoulders drooped. 'Take the main road that way,' she said in a flat monotone voice. 'Are you sure you can't wait? I don't see any smoke from where they would be.'

'I've messed up already.' Scout said in her efficient and regimented manner. 'I intend to follow instructions fully from now on.'

Mercy brushed down her clothes and then shrugged. 'I guess we will catch you up.'

Scout gave a stiff nod and then jogged up the road and out of sight.

Eban began to hum. He gathered up the curtain around the treasure and marched up the road a short distance. The others picked up what was left and followed.

The houses here were detached but smaller than the ones in the area near the library. The façades were just a mask of decay. The crumbling bricks and ivy clad walls were maintained to keep up the appearance of abandonment. Luca shook his head as he realised that Tropolis were not fooled by the disguise; they had intercepted light hearted chatter from two friends proving that this place was thriving away from the control of Tropolis.

Eban approached a low garden gate that been shut. 'This is as good as any,' he suggested, pushing the gate open and wandering up the path. He pulled down on the old-fashioned latch at the door and it swung open freely. 'Anyone home?' he called. There was no reply. He flicked the light switch and the hallway was flooded with light. 'Excellent!' Eban said triumphantly. 'They have power.' He walked into the first room. 'This way!' he called over his shoulder.

The room was dark but homely. Thick beams stretched across the whitewashed ceiling. The space was neatly furnished with a couple of soft chairs and a low table. In the fireplace there was a blackened stove, but it had no ashes inside. The window was just like all windows in the Campion settlement, it was covered in a thick blackout drape.

Eban put the curtain with all the salvaged equipment inside and pushed the table up against the wall. He started to pull out specific items and lay them out on the floor.

'Luca,' he said, 'That monitor can be plugged in over there.' He pointed to a socket. 'And that signal scanner you have, Mercy, needs to go next to it.'

Eban gave out instruction after instruction until all the sockets had been used up. He even used the neighbouring rooms for some items. He was particularly pleased with a few of the things that Kelsee had been able to save. There were two further radios and a lapel communicator. The battery power levels were very low on both radios, so they would take two valuable socket points. Eban set one up in the kitchen to charge whilst the other he kept close and turned onto channel six. The fuzzy voices spoke out occasionally. It seemed that the efforts of the Campion people were being rewarded as the fires were coming under control.

Luca fidgeted in the chair as he watched Eban decipher the codes on the two screens they had been able to save. The laptop had been damaged in the escape from the comms room and now the screen was a useless mash of colours and lines. Eban had managed to link most of the equipment to each other, but he was missing a few leads and had to keep walking from one room to the other to check.

'Go and make a drink or something,' Eban finally said. 'You know me, I could do with some food too.'

Luca wandered into the narrow kitchen where the girls were already sipping on hot chocolate. He inhaled the sweet smell as he searched the cupboards for more mugs.

Kelsee opened the drawer next to her and passed Luca a spoon. 'Is he done in there?'

'I have no idea!' Luca replied, his eyes wide. Kelsee laughed as she perched up on the worktop. It was refreshing to see her genuine smile. Eban had been right about not rushing into danger with Alard; Kelsee needed time and space to organise her own feelings. Mercy was ensuring that she had both. 'You could have made us some.'

'You seemed a bit busy.'

Mercy leaned forward and opened a cupboard. 'I suppose Eban is hungry.' The shelves were laden with many types of vegetables. 'There is some bread over there too. You should try that jam on toast.'

Luca raised his eyebrows.

'Here, I'll do it,' Kelsee said. 'It's no pumpkin soup, but it is one of my favourites.' Kelsee cut the bread into slices and then put them under the grill. 'And their jam is really good too. Lovely big strawberries in it.'

Eban rubbed his hands together at the sight of the full tray, with mugs of hot chocolate, plates of jam on toast and two crisp apples.

Luca crunched on the toast and could understand Kelsee's preference. 'Any joy?' Luca asked.

'Nothing,' Eban replied. 'I keep thinking that I have got through and then I get to another dead end. I think that there is a program at their end that is creating blocks as I go. Mmmm,' Eban took a bite of the toast, 'This is good!' Luca nodded. 'I've tried all direct routes in, but there are a few others yet to try.'

The radio sparked into life again. 'Captain Scout to control. Over.'

'Control, receiving.'

'Excellent work from all teams. Fire at the stores is now out. Sending the rest of the crew your way, sir. Over.'

'With a few more hands here, we will be in the same ...' The voice of the commander at the Library stopped suddenly. Luca got up to check the radio. It was still charging and seemed to be working. He held the radio to his ear but there was no noise at all.

'I'll check the other one,' Luca suggested getting up, then pointed to his food. 'That is my plate of toast. Don't you dare!'

Eban laughed. 'Make me some more whilst you are out there!'

Mercy and Kelsee stopped talking as soon as Luca walked into the kitchen.

'Was it something I said?' he asked reaching behind Kelsee's back for the radio.

'No!' Kelsee said, her cheeks turning red.

Luca switched the radio on and set it to channel six. There was no sound from this one either.

'I'll leave you two to it.' Luca marched back to Eban. 'Nothing on that one either.'

The radio burst into life again and the commander's voice rang out clearly. 'Control to all units: All personnel to the town hall immediately.' Then there was silence.

Luca frowned and leaned closer to the radio. 'That was odd.'

'I guess they have the fire under control at the library too.'

'No, wasn't he just saying to Debs that he wanted more people at the library or that it was nearly out before he cut off?' Luca frowned. 'And besides, they never end a message without saying *over*.'

Eban was fixated on the screen and busy typing something. 'I guess so,' he replied absently.

'Captain Scout responding. Can you repeat the command, or do you still want me to follow previous commands? Over.'

'Scout!' the commander interrupted angrily. 'All personnel to the town hall immediately.'

'Yes sir. Sorry to ask for clarification. I will be there as soon as possible. Over.'

Luca pointed to the radio. 'See. Scout said over.'

Mercy stood at the door. 'Did you hear that too? There was something wrong with that message.'

Luca reached for the lapel communicator. 'How does this communicator work?'

'Just use the radio,' Eban said.

'I want to talk to Scout, not anyone else. I'm not sure the radio system is secure. How does this work?'

Eban squeezed it between his fingers. 'Debs, are you there? Over.'

'Who is this? Over.' Scout replied.

Eban handed the lapel communicator to Luca.

'It's Luca. Over.'

'Oh, how have you got hold ... oh, was there a tapper in the comms room? Over.'

Luca looked at the communicator and assumed that is what the Campion named it.

'Yes. Where are you, over?'

'I saw the farm buildings, I think. Are they old barns? Mercy was right, there was no fire and no smoke. I think they are safe and hidden from attack. Anyway, I was called back to the town hall before I had a chance to investigate. Over.'

'I think you should be careful. That message was weird. Over.'

'The commander can be a bit grumpy sometimes, nothing I can't handle, over.'

'Alright,' Luca said reluctantly. 'Over.'

'Keep in touch. Over and out.'

Everyone sat in the lounge as Eban busied himself at the laptop. Nothing he tried seemed to get through the firewall and into Tropolis.

As the moments passed, Luca grew more agitated. He wanted to do something but was stuck watching Eban instead. The time dragged and Luca, uneasy with just sitting, went to the window. He pulled the drape aside and watched the distant flames from Alard's house. The roof had collapsed whilst the friends had been in the flint outhouse; the top floor must have fallen in soon after. The flames were now consuming what was left. The solid walls of the old building were keeping the fire contained and the isolation of the Brigadier's house meant that the fire was less likely to spread. Luca couldn't help thinking that if this had been Outside, a whole quarter would have been destroyed, but in Tropolis' fancy buildings the flames would have been extinguished in moments. Luca wanted Tropolis, or at least Hutchings and the ark to taste fire. He dropped his gaze. It was dangerous to think such things, but with the stink of burning lingering in the air, he couldn't escape his dark thoughts.

The tapper sprang to life abruptly. Scout's voice was hushed.

'Luca! I hope you are listening. Please don't reply. Just listen! Campion have been captured.'

Luca rushed for the tapper. Everyone in the room was still and silent as they listened to the whispered warning.

'The men from the Maglev are here. They have taken us hostage and are holding us in the library. They have weapons and are searching the village for anyone they can find. You have to get out. Get out now! Over and out.'

Chapter 5

Luca stared at the tapper in his hand and wanted to wake up. Surely, he had endured enough and it was his time to see some victory. The atmosphere was heavy with fear.

The screen blinked and flickered but Eban was not paying attention to it. Luca glanced at all they had set up and wanted to scream. They were so close.

'We've ... we've got to ... got to get out!' Kelsee said her voice trembling as she grabbed the document folder and held it close.

She had broken the silence that had held them.

Luca hissed. 'Not yet! Eban is nearly there.'

Eban shook his head. 'I'm not putting us in that kind of danger. I don't know how much longer I will be. I'm running out of ideas.'

Luca stepped forward. 'You stay here, and I'll hold them off.'

Mercy stood. 'No!' She reached out and grabbed Luca's arm. 'We work together, remember.' Mercy paced the small room. 'There must be a way to stop them. Only Atticus and Seth had weapons.'

Luca shoved the tapper in his pocket. 'From what I saw, Thickset was very happy to use them.'

Mercy met Luca's hard gaze. 'But they were the only ones with weapons. The other men, the ones from the dockside, they didn't have anything with them. We only need to over-power Atticus and Seth.' Luca glowered at Mercy. 'Thickset's name is Seth. You don't know who he has become.'

'He's a power-crazy thug who tried to kill me.'

Eban grabbed the radio and clipped it to his belt. 'This is ground level three, a residential settlement, but they wouldn't leave it unable to defend itself.'

Luca welcomed the change of tone. 'You think they have weapons too.'

Eban shrugged. 'Makes sense.'

The thought that he would be able to defend himself lifted some of the weight from Luca. He hadn't practiced in the shooting range for the endurance test. He glanced at Mercy and realised that she hadn't either. She covered her mouth with her hand.

'It's not as if we would know where to find them.' Luca said, his voice quiet and defeated. 'If we use the radio or tapper they'll know we are here and come looking for us.'

Mercy brushed down her clothes. 'Well, we can't leave them in danger. We know where they are being held, we just need to check the coast is clear before we speak to Debs. If she is with the other Campion leaders, surely they will know how we can help them.'

Kelsee looked shocked. 'You want to get weapons to hurt them?'

Mercy shook her head. 'Not at all.'

'Let's go!' Luca said.

Eban unplugged the radio that had been charging. 'Get the other one from the kitchen.' Kelsee dashed out. 'Have you got the tapper?' Luca nodded. 'I can't take any of this stuff. The laptop is useless without a screen, we'll just have to leave it here. How's that fire doing?'

'This house is safe from the flames,' Luca replied.

Within moments the friends were out on the street. The sun was already setting, and the daylight was fading but Luca knew that the mixture of smoke, twilight and Thickset's unfamiliarity with the settlement would favour them. They kept as close to the shadows as possible weaving their way down a back lane. Eban was certain that the little roads would merge somewhere in the centre of the village but getting away from the main thoroughfare would be wise.

The deserted houses seemed more barren than before. Luca wasn't sure if it really was that way or the knowledge that the inhabitants had been gathered in the library that made the village eerily still.

Luca ducked behind the wall that surrounded a small tarmacked area next to the library. There was one hi-vis clad Tropolite stood just outside the cracked glass door. There was no sign of any other Tropolites as Luca slowly approached the building half ruined by the flames. The library had only been single storey and had squatted low to the ground but looked even smaller now that the sloping roof was jagged and incomplete. The timbers were still smouldering from the fire but even though there were no flames Luca wondered just how safe it was for the people being held inside. The ceiling had crashed in so suddenly before, he hoped that the remaining structure was stable.

He gestured to the others to move closer. 'The front is blocked,' he whispered, 'There must be another way in.'

Luca climbed over the wall and dropped to the tarmac, keeping out of the guard's line of sight. The others followed. They crept to the back of the building. Luca's breath caught when he saw the paint peeled door. This was access to his mother's office, he was certain of it. He pressed his ear up against the woodwork and could hear muffled voices coming from the other side. He ushered the friends on; this would not be a safe way in. They skirted the rest of the building, keeping close to the walls. The very few low-level windows were blacked out, but Luca still tried each one for access. The majority of the windows seemed to be high up, presumably leaving the internal walls free for book shelves in the main reading space. Luca looked longingly at the possible access points that were out of reach. Further down the structure there was a retaining wall that held the earth back from the library's neigbour. He hurried to it and clambered up on the brickwork and leaned into the library wall. He shuffled along to the first window and tucked his fingers under the rim of the opening. It would not move.

'Be careful!' whispered Kelsee.

Luca reached down to Eban. 'Come and help.'

Eban hoisted himself onto the wall. When he was in place, they each took one of Mercy's hands and lifted her to the wall, and then Kelsee.

Luca indicated that Eban should start in the opposite direction. He smiled and nodded. Luca stretched to the second window. He desperately dug his fingers under the frame and pulled. It tilted a little. Finally, one that opened. He waved frantically at Eban to catch his attention and soon all four of them were gathered and waiting.

Kelsee took one edge and Luca the other. They pulled the window open.

The main library space was smoke blackened and half open to the sky. The ceiling had collapsed and large chunks of roofing that had not been consumed by the flames littered the floor, crushing chairs and tumbled down shelves. There was very little light, but Luca could make out the huddled forms of people in the far corner of the room. They were sat on the floor and any remaining chairs. Willow was at the far side, in her wheelchair. A line of blue-uniformed men fenced the others inside as if barricading them from the enemy. It was a desperate last stand and Luca battled against a sinking feeling of defeat.

Luca scanned their faces. Scout was nursing her wounded arm, sitting next to Willow.

'There is the guard out front but none in the library, Luca,' Eban whispered, reminding Luca to take action. 'Contact Debs now.'

Luca reached into his pocket and squeezed the tapper. Debs suddenly sat up straight.

'Debs,' Luca whispered. 'We need to get you out.'

She reached up to her shoulder. 'I told you to leave!'

'We can't leave Campion like this.' Luca replied. 'Where are the weapons?'

'The same two men, Atticus and Seth – you know, Thickset – they have them. In the room next to me.'

'Not those weapons – the ones to defend ground level three.'

Debs shifted forward. Luca stared as she leaned across Willow and reached out to the older man that Luca thought of as the commander. There was a hurried conversation. The commander smirked a little and nodded before saying something back to Debs.

'Luca. You've got to be careful. Do you promise?'

Luca frowned at Debs. 'I'm not a child. Don't treat me like one. Where are they?'

'In the church bell tower. But how are you ...'

There was movement at the main door. A Tropolite came running in.

'Sergeant sir, I found something!' he yelled at the top of his voice.

A moment later Atticus strolled in, wiping his mouth on the back of his hand. Thickset followed close behind, rifle in one hand and a half-eaten cake in the other.

'Sergeant Atticus, sir. We've found this and a whole load of gear set up in one of the houses near a burn out. The lights were on, but no-one was home.'

'Really?' Atticus replied looking at his captors. 'Now what would a group of ancient misfits want with this kind of gear?'

Atticus marched over to Debs and grabbed her by her injured arm. 'Stop complaining!' He dragged her to the centre of the room and threw her to the floor. 'What is a woman doing in an army with all these old men?'

Debs took a deep breath and got to her feet. 'This is not an army. How many times do I need to tell you that?'

Thickset rushed forward and carelessly shoved the tip of his rifle against her chin forcing her to stare at the damaged rafters. 'Show some respect!'

'Leave her alone!' the commander cried out.

Debs stood completely still.

Atticus began to circle Debs and Thickset. He clenched his hands behind his back. 'He wants me to leave you alone. I have to ask myself why. Why should I leave you alone? Is it because you are the weakest link in their defences? You are, after all, just a woman. Is it because you don't know anything important?' Atticus shook his head. 'I have been thinking,' he said standing very close to her. 'I think I might have seen you before. In fact, I know I've seen you before.' He prodded her arm. She winced. He then pulled on the blood-stained sleeve. 'That was done from a bullet. From a bullet from my rifle. I shot you this morning.'

Debs raised her head a little higher but didn't say a word.

'I knew it. I thought I had got one of you.' Atticus laughed cruelly. 'The thing is, I would have much preferred to get one of those competitors, I'm sure you know what I mean.'

'They are long gone,' Debs said filling the silence.

'Really? I didn't even ask you about them.' Atticus reached over to the Tropolite. 'What's this you found?' Atticus snatched the item from the man's hands. It was flat and rectangular. It was only a moment later that Luca realised what he had. Atticus pulled it open and artificial light shone on his face. There were a useless mash of colours and lines on the screen.

Luca turned to Eban who had covered his mouth. Luca vigorously shook his head as his eyes widened. All of their equipment had been found.

'I know that one of those competitors was a bit of a whizz on the gadgets. I know that he cheated his way through to the next round when I wanted him dead.'

'I wanted him dead too.' Thickset growled.

'Yes. I know,' Atticus said, 'You didn't manage to get that right either.'

Thickset's lip curled.

'Now, now, enough of that!' Atticus said batting away his comment. He looked at the screen and turned the laptop over. 'Well this wasn't worth gleaning!' He threw the machine at the wall where the casing smashed, the screen separated from the main body and a blue spark emitted as it hit. Atticus licked his lips and smiled. 'Where are they?'

'They're gone. They didn't come to Campion with me.'

'But they were here. They were hiding up in that house with all their toys. What are they doing?'

'They were never here. I don't know where they are now. Long gone, I expect.' Debs tried to look at Atticus. 'All that stuff is mine. All those computers and gear, it's all mine.' Debs sighed. 'They might have found it useful if they had been here, but they just want to be free.'

'Free!' Atticus said swiping the rifle away from Debs chin. He leaned in very close but spoke even louder than before. 'I saw what freedom looked like!'

Luca was surprised that Debs didn't flinch. He was grateful for her cover story and hoped that Atticus had believed her.

Atticus continued. 'I saw them all heading off to conquer Tropolis. How do you think that will go, eh?' He didn't wait for Debs to answer. 'Your lovely smoke signals showed me the place that Tropolis wanted to destroy. I'm here to make sure that happens.' He moved away slightly. 'I'm glad there are more people here than I thought there would be. More coins in my coffer that way. I thought that this place would be deserted and that you had all gone to Tropolis for your freedom.' He laughed sarcastically. 'Although your lot seems to be full of weaklings. Is that why you came here? Were you going to defend them? I guess, I'll have to be the one that delivers you to the city instead. I'm sure that Tropolis would make you very welcome.' He sneered. 'So welcome that you could be the making of me.' He stood in front of the people grouped in the corner and laughed at their misfortune. 'You were not able to defend yourselves, but Tropolis need not know that. Your sorry version of hidden life wouldn't be able to hold me back. You are pathetic. You had to send out your finest on the boats to do your fighting for you, and I have to say, they weren't that fine. They won't be coming back.' He bounced on his toes rubbing his hands together. 'And they left you weak and ill guarded, I'm just ensuring that this opportunity doesn't get missed.'

'You won't get anything from Tropolis,' Debs said bravely. 'Tropolis will fall.'

The people seemed to stir, and courage was mounting.

Atticus stepped back from them. But laughed loudly. 'No madam, you will fall. Had you known where those kids were it might have been different, you see, I want them. But since you are as useless as you look...' He turned to Thickset. 'Shoot her.'

Thickset slowly raised the rifle to Debs' chest. Debs looked straight into Seth's eyes.

'What are you waiting for?' Atticus sneered. 'Shoot her!'

Thickset continued to hesitate, so Atticus reached round, placed his hand over Seth's and squeezed the trigger.

A sharp bang filled the room and Debs body was thrown backwards to the ground.

Kelsee let out a yelp but it was hidden in the hiss of gasps and cries from the crowd.

Luca wanted to turn away from the revulsion before him. He watched as a blood flowed through Debs' clothes and began to pool on the floor. He hoped that this was some mistake, but she lay unnaturally still. He turned to Eban whose eyes were wide in horror.

The bullet had easily hit its mark and punched a way through her heart killing her instantly.

Atticus, completely at ease faced the crowd again. 'Shut up the lot of you! Let that be a lesson to all of you ring leaders. Do you want to be next?' A deadly silence fell.

Luca looked at the statue-like form of Thickset. His eyes were wide and his face pale. The rifle was still raised and pointing at the remembrance of a person who had stood there before. The shaft was shaking.

'You,' Atticus said pointing at the Tropolite that had bought the laptop to him. 'Take one of your mates and stake out that house. If they are still here, I want them caught.'

Atticus turned to march out of the room.

'Wait!' a lone female spoke out. Luca's breath caught – his mother had spoken. 'Please, we can't stay in this building. It isn't safe.

'As if I care!' Atticus laughed and waved away the request with a swipe of his hand. He began to walk away.

Willow called after him. 'If you are keeping us here, we'll need blankets. We are exposed to the elements.'

'Seth! Come here!' Atticus commanded over his shoulder as he disappeared into the dry and safe back office. Seth obeyed, still trembling.

The commander stepped forward and reached for Debs' lifeless body. He placed his hand at her neck in the vain hope of finding a pulse and a few moments later, he lowered his head. He quickly pulled at the lapel communicator and tucked in into his hand.

'Captain Scout is dead,' he whispered. 'I don't know what you can do, but please help us.'

Chapter 6

Mercy wiped the tears from her face with her sleeve. Kelsee was still shaking as Luca helped her off the wall.

'She didn't deserve to die,' Kelsee muttered half to herself.

'She sacrificed herself so that we could live,' Luca said holding her close. 'She was incredibly brave. I'll never forget what she did for us.'

Eban was strangely quiet. Luca knew that Debs had been one of the Campion leaders that Eban had particularly warmed to. He tried to offer some support to his friend with a smile but did not know what he could say to make it any easier.

Mercy whispered urgently. 'We need to find that bell tower.'

Luca was a little surprised at Mercy's determination. She had always been such a peace-loving person in the past, never resorting to violence. She always seemed to find another way to resolve a matter. This was, perhaps, not one of those times. Luca could feel his muscles tense.

'Are you alright?' Kelsee whispered.

Luca nodded. He turned to Mercy. 'Let's go. Do you know what a church looks like?'

Mercy shook her head. 'But I do know what a tower is, and I think we passed one earlier.'

The sun had dipped below the roof line of the houses and the light was fading fast. The clouds were beginning to gleam a golden orange that made Luca think of the flames that had brought them here.

Mercy led them through the back streets. She occasionally spoke quietly to Eban who walked beside her. They were extra cautious at every corner and junction, even though it seemed logical that Atticus' men would head towards Alard's burnt out house since that is where they would be watching all the gear that the friends had left.

Luca took Kelsee's hand. She was cold. 'Do up your jacket.' Luca said.

'I can't.' Kelsee replied shivering a little. 'The papers from my grandfather's house are in my inside pocket and they are too bulky.'

'I can carry them,' Luca offered.

'No!' Kelsee replied quickly. Luca was taken aback. Kelsee softened her tone. 'I want to keep them safe. I know he wasn't to blame for what has happened recently, but all this has occurred because of what he started.' Kelsee lowered her gaze and pulled her jacket tighter around herself. 'I feel like I have some responsibility to these people, to your people and to mine. They didn't know him like I did. He was all I had left.'

'It isn't your fault.' Luca said quietly.

'I know, but it feels like the only thing that I can do to help at the moment.' Kelsee squeezed his hand. 'I'm so glad that I have you to help me, but with the communication and computer stuff found, this might be all we have.'

'We have radios and the tapper,' Luca began, hoping that they would help, but he knew that there was no way of resurrecting and restoring that video with what little they had.

Luca's stomach churned as he began to think about how close they had been to breakthrough. If only Eban had worked faster and found a way into the Network or the Tropolis computers. If only he had been more able to help out. Luca ran his fingers through his hair and then allowed the weight of his own inadequacy to hunch his shoulders. He had been useless and impatient in the house and had taken to staring out of the window instead of helping.

Luca gasped. The phrase that the Tropolite man with the laptop had used hit Luca in the chest. *The lights were on, but no-one was home.* Luca had pulled back the blackout drapes to stare at the burning building, but he had never closed them. Their communications gear was lost because he had not behaved like the Campion people, instead he had invited the Tropolite guard right in.

Luca wiped the sweat from his forehead. His hand was trembling.

'What is it?' Kelsee asked.

Luca wanted to hide away. His thoughts hastily confirmed that he was to blame not just for the broken laptop but for everything else. It was all his fault that they were now being hunted, that the video would not be aired, that the Outsiders would never be welcome in Tropolis and that Captain Debs Scout was dead.

Luca let go of Kelsee's hand and pulled his own jacket close to him. He did his best to offer a smile but knew from the frown Kelsee gave him that he had failed to cover his shame. He lifted the hood.

'Where's that church?' he hissed. There was an urgency that Luca had not felt before. Perhaps finding the weapons and freeing the Campion people would somehow vindicate him for his part in Debs' death.

'There!' Mercy said, turning to Luca and Kelsee. She was pointing at a tower that peeked over a bank of dark evergreen trees. Mercy scratched her cheek and tilted her head to one side.

'That could be the place,' Luca said trying to deflect Mercy's confusion.

The friends approached.

A rough flint wall circled the lonely building. Long grass that was dying away and tall weeds that had been left undisturbed for years, extended across the footpath in a tangled mess. The undergrowth appeared even thicker at the edges of the tumble-down entrance where at the break in the wall stood an old wooden shelter. It had been left unused and was now in a bad state of disrepair. The shelter's tiny pitched roof had tiles missing and was covered in moss. Luca could tell that this particular plot, and even the larger building had not been carefully maintained to look deserted; it really was.

They trampled the weeds and pushed through the gate.

The ancient trees dotted the grassed area interspersed with headstones. The grass here was also dying back and lay in unordered swathes of differing greens and browns. It seemed quieter under the shade of the trees, as if their branches hushed the world on the other side.

When Luca looked up he saw the church was silhouetted against the fading red sky. It's sturdy stone walls were covered with creeping ivy that twisted up onto the slate roof. They approached the building from the side, passing the tall tower before reaching the lower roofed section. Tall, arched windows, which were segmented with abstract shapes, stood guard over the wide doorway.

'It is so peaceful here,' Mercy commented with a gentle smile.

Kelsee shook her head. 'Let's just get inside.'

Ornate iron hinges almost stretched the entire width of the double doors. The rain that had caused them to drip rust on the light-coloured wood had, over time, stained it with dark tears. Eban took hold of the latch, depressed it and pushed the door.

The door shifted just a little to begin with as the hinges had been set for a long time. A deep creak echoed in the room beyond and the bottom of the door rubbed against the floor.

The smell of damp and dust wafted out on a cold draft and was so acute that it made Luca's nose tingle. Every small sound seemed to be amplified in the dark church.

Luca reached into his pocket and pulled out the torch as they cautiously entered.

He slowly swept the space with the beam of light. Many long wooden bench seats had been pushed up to one side, some of which were balanced on others. There were also a couple of stacks of broken chairs. On a window sill was a large pile of dusty books; their pages were dirt stained and wavy from damp. Several small windows down both sides of the room punctured the thick stone walls, but they had not been covered in the Campion curtains. At the far end, in a slightly elevated position, was a much larger window. Luca lifted the torch beam to find that it stretched high into the roof space of the gable end. The massive arched glass was fragmented, just as all the other panes were.

Mercy stepped further into the room and stared up into the darkened ceiling. 'It's beautiful!' she whispered.

Kelsee had wandered over to a door at one side. She squeezed past the benches and was lifting a few chairs out of the way. 'The tower should be through this way.'

She opened it and as it pushed against one of the benches, a loud screech filled the hall. Mercy jumped, laughed to herself and then hurried over to help. They cleared the benches away and opened the door wide enough for them to enter.

Luca was expecting to see a flight of stairs but instead he was faced with dark square room and a single swaying rope suspended from an untidy wooden ceiling. An unnerving draught whistled from somewhere above and the thick cobwebs billowed in the gentle breeze that filtered down. Luca stepped into the middle of the room and saw that the rope came through a hatch in the ceiling. Luca shone the light through the hole and saw that the other end of the rope hung from a number of large metal mechanisms, one of which was hollow and rocked slightly.

'This is the bell tower. I think that rope rings the bell,' Luca said. He turned and quickly pulled Kelsee's hand from the thick cord. 'It will be best not to touch it.'

A dust covered ladder was hung from the wall on mis-shapen brackets.

'There is nothing but this rope here,' Kelsee said. 'Where are the weapons?'

Eban and Luca had already lifted the ladder and had carefully manoeuvred it to so that the top end rested at the edge of the hatch.

'You go,' Luca said standing at the foot of the ladder.

Eban pulled out his own torch and climbed. The rungs of the ladder hummed as his feet rubbed against them. He shone the beam through the hatch and followed.

A few moments later Eban appeared back at the hatch. 'There are a few boxes,' he called down, 'But that's all.' Eban shifted around above them, his feet scraping on the grit and dirt from above. 'No rifles.'

'Pass us the boxes,' Luca said.

Kelsee climbed up the ladder and collected what Eban had deposited by the hatch. She passed them down to Luca who handed them to Mercy.

'That's all there is,' Eban said after he had passed the third cardboard box to Kelsee. 'This one's a bit fragile.' Luca was disappointed. None of these boxes were big enough for a rifle.

Mercy unfolded the flaps and they all gathered around.

The first box was packed tightly with smaller plastic containers and packaging chips. Mercy pulled one container out and handed it to Eban. She then gave one to each of the friends.

Luca unclipped the lid and opened it. It was full of silver coloured metal cylinders, about the length of his little finger. He took one in his hand. It was cold to touch but light. It felt as if it contained a tiny amount of liquid.

Mercy reached further inside the box. She lifted out a smaller card container and opened it. This box contained packets of sealed batteries.

Eban pulled the second box open. Luca could see that it contained more of the same plastic containers alongside some oddly shaped, almost rectangular, black plastic components. Eban turned one over in his hand. It was small enough to sit on his palm. There were round buttons on either side that, when depressed, pushed in two simple plastic catches. This object obviously fixed into something

Luca reached quickly for the third and final box. This box was damaged, and damp had caused the card to rot away. Luca opened the top and the flap tore away in his hand. Whatever this box contained was hidden by packaging chips. He dipped his hand inside and pulled out what looked like a bright yellow plastic gun. It was bulky and could have been childlike if the handgrip area wasn't designed for an adult's hand.

The barrel had a semi-circular section cut from it. Eban passed the thing he was holding to Luca.

'Try this in the end,' Eban suggested.

The component slotted in easily and the catches locked into place. Luca nodded and smiled widely.

He turned his hand gun shaped object in his hand and gave it to Eban. He tipped the box over and riffled through the chips. He passed the other yellow guns to the friends. There were twelve handsets.

Eban was busy studying the gun in his hand. There was a lever near the top that could either be moved to S or T. He twisted it round so that it pointed at S and then noticed the small light below the shaft. 'Those batteries fit in this,' Eban said squeezing the tabs on the handle. A narrow section popped out. 'Here, they go in here.'

Eban opened a battery pack and connected a battery.

He pointed the barrel to the corner.

'You'll make too much noise!' Kelsee said.

'There aren't any bullets in this thing. Watch.'

Eban pulled the trigger and a bright spark of blue danced across the electrodes at the end of the barrel. 'This is a stun gun,' he said as he flipped the switch at the top. He pulled the trigger again. A red laser light dot appeared at the target then there was a quiet pop as two projectiles shot into the corner followed by a clicking noise.

Eban unclipped the battery pack and pulled on the fine wires that had uncoiled. At the end of them were two barbed pins. 'It's a taser, a weapon that won't kill but give a nasty shock.' Eban nodded with a determined expression. 'It will be enough if we can get these to them.'

Mercy slouched. 'We all saw what Atticus did,' she said. 'He doesn't care who he hurts, and he hurts anyone who knows where we are.'

'Can we just go back to the library and throw them in?' Kelsee suggested.

Eban shook his head. 'That sounds like it might work but is a bit too haphazard. What if the guards see?'

Kelsee sat up tall. 'Then I'll take them in.' She raised her hand as Luca was about to protest. 'Atticus knows who I am, and I could be a valuable hostage to him. I could just walk right in. He will be happy to have me. Then, once I am in, I can easily escape him because Campion will overpower them.'

Luca balled his fists. He was not going to let Kelsee cover for his mistakes. 'And what do you suppose will be the first thing they do when they capture you?' Luca said aggressively.

Kelsee leaned away from him. 'They'll take me to the Campion people.'

'Wrong!' Luca replied through tight lips. 'They will search you and take the tasers from you, and then you will be more ammo for him.' Luca shook his head. 'You are not going!'

'Woah!' Eban said patting the air. 'Luca, back off!' He put his hand on Luca's shoulder. 'Kelsee was making a suggestion, that is all. What is going on with you right now?'

Luca pulled away and puffed out a breath. 'I'm just tired.' Eban was the last person he wanted to admit his guilt to. If he had been more careful he could have been eating jam with Eban right now, laughing at the simplicity of showing the message from the peace of Campion ground level three. Eban could have saved everyone, including Debs.

'We should get these tasers ready to go,' Eban said seemingly unaware that Luca was to blame. 'We can have a think about how to get them into the library.'

When all the tasers were armed Mercy insisted that everyone rest. Kelsee wanted to stay inside the bell tower room and even though it was just as cold as the main hall, the lower ceiling and tighter space made it appear cosier. The Outsider in Luca and Eban arranged the unfolded boxes in such a way that, along with the packing chips, they were able to stay relatively warm. The sound of the patter of gentle rain floated down the tower.

Mercy was happy to take the first watch and sat facing the door, a loaded taser in her hand. It seemed an unreconcilable image to Luca, since Mercy would never use such a weapon. He hoped that the church would be a safe place to hide until they had a plan.

It was still dark when Eban woke him. Luca rubbed his eyes and stretched. He felt a little better from his sleep until the memory of where they were and what he had made happen came back to mind. He carefully slipped out from under the cardboard packing and flexed his back. It had been a long time since he had slept on the floor. Eban patted him on the back and laid down quietly. His eyes were closed in seconds and he was breathing deeply very soon after.

Luca peered over at Kelsee. He flicked his torch on for a moment. She looked peaceful and trouble free, her wild curly hair framed her face – a face that Luca was certain was more angular than before. It was wrong that she was also suffering because of him. He paused and listened to the night; gentle breathing, the patter of rain and the soft brushing of the rope against the wall as it swayed slightly. The stillness of the night was all consuming. He hadn't had time alone for a while and the prospect frightened him. He wasn't sure he wanted to really think about all that was going on. He spotted the edge of the document folder poking out from

Kelsee's jacket that she had laid over herself as a blanket. Luca reached over and gently pulled at it. Kelsee had rolled the documents to fit into her pocket so Luca had to prise them out trying not to disturb her.

After he had released them, he uncurled them by rolling them the opposite way and opened the folder.

It wasn't a huge stack of papers but the top couple of sheets had been stamped with an official Tropolite seal.

On flicking through, there appeared to be very few pages that a person from Outside would understand. There were details of new policies and many references to people using just their initials and things he had no knowledge of. These were all nonsense to him. In the end Luca found that he was just scanning the pages for things that he would recognise.

There were a few pages about halfway through the stack that offered details of Emundabit, although these were very vague. When he checked, these were notes taken from a meeting dating back ten years or so. Perhaps the vagueness was due to this being the ideas or planning meeting. There was talk of *eradicating the enemy and preserving provision for Tropolis* had they been put under siege. Luca smirked. The thought of Tropolis coming under siege would have been unfounded that far back. Even now it seemed it was completely unlikely, but perhaps Tropolis was thinking that this could be a possibility and was, after all, almost their current situation. The paragraphs that followed gave a bare bones structure to the Emundabit plan. A large storage facility to sustain life, the protection of the Tropolite people by the security personnel and brief action plan to attack. The security would require specific training and need strong and healthy candidates. The plan to attack had been suggested by MH, but been vetoed by HB. Luca folded the top corner of this sheet. Mara Hutchings and Harland Barret had disagreed on the outworking of Emundabit.

Several others had been at the meeting and their initials had been recorded in the notes. It seemed that Harland had the support of many of them when it went to vote. However,

Hutchings had been instructed, as personal assistant to Harland, to source statistics, ideas, pricings and availability of a storage facility for Tropolis. The next meeting would be scheduled for the following month and a full investigation into the possibility of attack was to be presented.

Luca hurriedly turned the page. He was pleased to find that the notes from the next meeting were also available. The agenda contained points on deciding and accessing secure words used over the Network for Tropolis security, presentation of findings regarding future welfare of Tropolis and emigration/defection. The presentation notes had been printed for Harland and his board to discuss. There were statistics of Tropolites that had gone missing from the database. A few had been taken into custody after asking to leave Tropolis. These were asterisked in red pen and scribbled notes written against them, *"Consultant ... paediatrician ... chairman of the board"*. Luca read on.

"When asked the reason for leaving and where they were going, they refused to answer." *Asked*. The word *asked* was underlined and a large question mark was placed next to this statement. The scribble next to it made Luca shiver. *"Cold cell and white torture"*. Luca placed the paper back on the pile as if it were contaminated with poison. Tropolis had tortured their own people, even someone they knew, from their own staff, in their method of *asking*. No wonder this paper had been locked away in the safe.

Luca needed to know what information this had produced. He gingerly read on.

Tropolis had learned that there were people living apart from Tropolis control, free from their influence and surviving the fatigue. But they had also found that there was an organisation that was helping others to escape along with an initial investigation into said organisation.

A defined line was drawn under this last statement several times and it seemed that the meeting didn't progress that well from this point as many had to be asked to leave the room and wait outside. *MEETING ABORTED* was written in block capitals.

The next sheet of paper contained the notes of the subsequent meeting a month later. There was very little that interested Luca and he turned the page lazily. It was only as he scanned the names at the end of the document that he realised that the entire board had changed, only HB and MH were repeated initials.

Luca sat very still for a moment. He couldn't believe what he was thinking. Had Harland *removed* everyone from the board that had heard of the torture and the place that was Tropolis free? He quickly checked for other meetings. As he flicked through he found a couple of copied black and white maps, their details lost a little and faded, but several crosses marked different locations. Further on there were other meeting notes, but those original names were gone forever.

Luca slouched against the wall. He was certain that the board had been hearing about Campion and that they had been deleted from Tropolis life. He wondered about those that had helped Tropolites to escape and suddenly thought of Alec.

Alec! Why hadn't he thought about Alec? They may not have all the computers and comms gear, but they did have Alec in Tropolis. If they could contact him, perhaps he could access the video in the media suite.

There must be a way of contacting the tower. Luca regretted not paying attention to the radio that Debs had used to contact the tower before. He unclipped the radio and turned the volume down low. He listened intently for any sound. Channel six was silent, but he didn't expect anything different. He turned to another channel, working through them methodically, but there were no other voices to be heard. It was very early in the morning and Luca convinced himself that everyone would be asleep.

Luca pulled the tapper from his pocket. And looked at it closely. He knew that he just needed to tap the top and he would be able to contact Scout's radio. Of course, Scouts radio needed to stay silent and Luca didn't want to put either themselves or those incarcerated in the library in even more danger, but there must be a way of contacting the sea forts with it. He had seen Major Thomas use one and knew there must be Campion staff at the forts. These communicators were for longer distance, if only he could get it to work.

A squeak came from outside. Luca picked up the taser and got to his feet. It was probably a mouse. Luca waited. The deep creak of the church door being opened echoed around the main hall. Luca's heart raced as he stood in front of his friends and faced the tiny door before him. They hadn't considered that this cosy room offered no escape. He kicked Eban who quickly stirred and sat up. Luca turned and hastily beckoned him to hush with a finger to his lips. Eban picked up a second taser and stood his ground next to Luca. There was no time to wake the girls. The door handle turned, Luca and Eban aimed their weapons and spots of red light flickered on the wood panel. The latch clicked, and the door slowly edged open towards them.

Chapter 7

Something banged at the door and it flung open.

Willow cursed and then threw her hands in the air. 'Don't shoot!' she called loudly. 'Campion friend!'

Luca's red target beam disappeared into the semi dark hall, aimed at a standing height but somewhere over Willow's head and completely missing the mark.

The sudden gust stirred the papers laying on the floor and they scattered.

Mercy woke with a start and Kelsee screamed hiding behind her jacket that she had raised to her face.

'Shhh!' Willow said, 'We don't want them to find you.'

Eban lowered the taser. 'What are you doing here?' He reached over to Luca and pushed the weapon down.

Luca stepped forward. His mother leaned forward, but Luca raised the taser and pushed past her. He shook his head as he peered outside. He wanted to check that she was alone. She blinked slowly and sighed.

'I came to help,' she said with a hint of sadness.

Luca ran his hand through his hair. 'Um, why?'

Mercy tutted. 'How did you get out? Are Campion in control again?'

Willow wheeled herself into the room. Weeds trailed from her chair where she had picked her way up the path to the church.

Kelsee put her coat back on and scurried forward to gather up the papers. She shuffled them into a pile but paused at the sheet with the folded corner. She looked up at Luca who closed the door behind Willow, raised her eyebrows at him and tilted her head in question. He nodded at her. As she lifted other papers she seemed to be scanning them for more information, now knowing that they were of use. Luca saw Kelsee pause as she looked at one yellowed sheet. She folded it over in her hand and stuffed in into her pocket before replacing the folder inside her jacket.

Willow had several folded blankets on her knees and a large bag stuffed with even more hanging from the wheelchair handles. 'Campion are still being held,' Willow began. Luca bit down on his lip. 'But,' she had obviously sensed Luca's suspicion, 'I convinced those Tropolites to let me go and get blankets. The library is cold, and the rain only made it worse. I told them that they need hostages that are alive if they want to impress their superiors.' Willow raised her hands. 'What can someone like me do? It isn't as if I could be any danger. I think I proved to them that I'm the most harmless!'

'Were you followed?' Luca asked, although he had already checked outside.

'No.' Willow huffed. 'There's only a few of them, and they are down two because they are watching the house with the gear they found. There is no way to spare any more when they have a library full of people.'

'How did you get out?' Mercy asked.

'The one with the gun, the younger one,' Willow began.

'Thickset?' questioned Luca.

Willow shrugged. 'I suppose. He was on guard in the early hours and virtually wheeled me to the door.' She patted the blankets on her lap. 'He told me to go and get these, but to be back before his watch ended.'

'So, what are you doing here then?' Luca asked scowling at her.

'It's where they said the weapons were kept. I heard the tapper communication. I thought, if you had left, I could find the weapons and bring them to Campion.'

'You would have had difficulty,' Luca replied meanly. 'They were up there.' He pointed to the hatch.

Willow smiled at her son. 'Then I'm glad that you are braver than me and stuck around to help.'

Mercy reached forward and touched Willow's hand. 'Bravery can only be measured because of courage. I'd say that you have had courage in leaving the library and coming here.'

'And I think,' Eban said laughing to himself, 'That we have just found a way of getting these weapons into the hands of Campion.' He patted the pile of blankets on Willow's lap. 'I think that those Tropolites may have underestimated you! You could be far from harmless.'

Willow nodded. 'I'm happy to take them back. I don't intend for Campion to be under Tropolite control.' She scowled at Kelsee before turning to Luca. 'I thought I'd never find it again, that passion to want to see change. I was so stuck. I'm so sorry.'

'For what exactly?' Luca asked with his arms folded.

'I'm sorry for not coming back to you, but at the same time so proud of who you have become. I heard them talking about what happened in the prize and what you did. They hate you,' Willow said her eyes bright, 'Really hate you.' She clasped her hands on her lap and smiled. 'I guess I'm grateful that even though I made the mistake, you discovered who you were without me.' She looked at her hands. 'You found who you were and have helped me resurrect who I was.' She glanced at Luca. 'I'm sorry that I hid away, frightened to even leave the library, terrified that real life would destroy me all over again. When in fact, I was destroying myself.' She reached for Luca, but he backed away. She paused for a moment, nodded at his response and lowered her hand. 'I can't change what has happened. I know what I did was wrong.' She glanced towards Mercy, 'I lacked courage. But I can only leave that behind and move on. Please forgive me from the past, Luca, and let me have a future. I want to be free.' She extended her hand towards him again. 'I believe this is the right choice.'

A single tear rolled down Luca's cheek. He had challenged her to not make the good choice but make the right one when he had left her at the library before. She had remembered his words. He wiped his face and then grabbed her hand. 'I forgive you, mum.' He could feel a weight lift from his shoulders and the tightening in his chest loosen. This was the right choice for him too.

She pulled him close and hugged him. 'Thank you!' she whispered in his ear.

After a few moments Eban interrupted. 'I think we need to get these to Campion.' Hanging from his forefinger were three taser guns. 'We have twelve. How many will be enough?'

'You must keep some back,' Willow said. 'You must stay safe.' She took two of the tasers and tucked them down the side of her chair. 'We'll have Campion back in control in no time.'

'I don't think we will be able to go with you,' Luca said. 'The Campion forces, alongside those from Outside are on the brink of entering Tropolis. They can't get in and need our help. Tropolis are fighting back.'

Willow sighed. 'Tropolis will never let them in. They should have just moved those from Outside to the Campion villages. That way, the fatigue would be gone from our communities and we would be strong.'

Luca shook his head. 'They haven't gone to them to conquer them, but to make them well.'

'You want Tropolis to be stronger?' Willow sat back in her chair.

'You don't get it!' Luca said rubbing his forehead. 'Why does there have to be a them and us? Those people are ill too.'

Eban loaded a couple more tasers into the bag hanging from Willow's chair and tucked others into the folds of the blankets. 'You have seen what Tropolis do.'

Willow nodded. 'And experienced it!'

'Exactly!' Eban said. 'But that isn't who Tropolis are. That is only the leadership, the ruling authority. That is the power that they wield.' Eban looked at Willow in the face. 'I know you have thought that Harland Barret was to blame.' Willow glanced at Kelsee. 'But he is dead, and we know that it wasn't all his fault.' Kelsee shifted uncomfortably.

'You don't know him like I did. He raised me,' Kelsee said defensively. 'You only know a very small part of him.' She sighed. 'And like Eban said, he's dead now, so please don't accuse him of everything that has gone bad for you because we don't know how much is his fault and how much of it is Hutchings.'

Eban responded to Kelsee's distress. 'There are other powers in Tropolis that have dictated how it has been run for years, but the rest of Tropolis is dying, they aren't that different to the rest of us.'

Willow looked at Kelsee with narrowed eyes.

Luca stepped in front of Kelsee. 'You need to understand that if we go to them and show them compassion, if we bring relief from their suffering ...'

Willow rubbed her brow. 'They are not suffering!'

Luca raised his voice slightly. 'They are suffering. They have fatigue, but they are also frightened and are just as abandoned as Outside. They need our compassion to burn for them. Without us they won't survive.'

Willow raised her chin. 'Have you ever thought that we would be better without them?'

Luca huffed. 'Yes.' He paused. 'But it won't be the fatigue that gets them. They are all set to die. The new authority in Tropolis has already signed their death papers.' Luca sighed. 'You have seen the violent fires burning in your own community. The leader of Tropolis will continue to attack until you are all dead. I've seen her, she will not leave you alone any longer. She knows that Campion and Outside are coming after her. She has to destroy us before we destroy her.'

Willow sagged in her chair. 'But you said that Campion and Outside can't get in. We can't win this.'

'We can.' Luca grabbed Kelsee's hand and pulled her close. 'Tropolites can be given sight again. Kelsee has seen what the powers of Tropolite leadership has done and she wants it to change.'

'And I,' Kelsee said looking to Luca, 'Have found who I can be and should be. I know that the leaders have done terrible things to hurt you. I'm sorry that they separated you from Luca and that you have had to hide away. I can't tell you how sorry I am.'

'That is only one girl.'

'But this isn't just any girl,' Luca replied. He wanted to shout out triumphantly that this is Kelsee Barret and she has more influence than even she knows about. He swallowed and stayed silent.

'Outside and Campion were united,' Mercy said, 'When they met each other. They have learned to work together already. What could happen if the people of Tropolis were able to meet them?' Mercy pushed her hands in her pockets. 'We had sent a message to the people telling them to trust us and that we were bringing the cure to them, but the video was tampered with and they now think we are attacking. They are stopping us from entering because they don't know the truth.'

Eban shuffled his feet. 'We were trying to get hold of that video and let them see what the Network had done to it, then using the comms gear from Alard's place restore it to the original message. But that is impossible without computer access.'

Luca turned and smiled at Eban. 'I remembered something before mum turned up. We have an inside man. Alec.'

Eban rubbed his hands together. 'Can he get to the video?'

'He kind of had access to the media suite before. We just need to communicate with him.'

'How did he get you out safely and into Campion?' Willow asked.

Luca raised his hand. 'He never said. But he must have communicated with Campion because they picked us up.'

'Then contact the tower and get them to send a message.' Willow said. 'You have a tapper, right?

'How?' Luca handed the lapel communicator to Willow.

She twisted the top section. 'Tower? Come in tower.'

'Tower responding. Please state your name and location. Over'

Willow spoke confidently. 'This is ground level three, close to the church tower. Over'

'Is that you Debs? Over.'

Guilt washed over Luca and his hands began to tremble.

Willow continued. 'No, it is not. We need you to get a message to someone in Tropolis that you have been in contact with in the past. His name is Alec and he has been sending Tropolites to Campion. Can you do that?'

'That would be classified information. Over.'

Luca thought he recognised the voice from the tower. He reached over to the tapper. 'Is this Captain Scout's brother? Over'

'Who is this? Is she alright? I've not heard from her since yesterday and she said she'd keep me informed. Over.'

'I'm sorry.' Luca took a deep breath. 'There have been some complications at ground level three. There are two men here from the Tropolite army and some other Tropolite workers that have come from attacking Outside. They have captured the people of ground level three.' Luca swallowed hard but knew he had to break the news. 'Debs was with those they took. They shot her. She was defending the Campion people and us. She died. I'm so sorry.' Luca wished he could say more but words failed him. He lowered his gaze to the floor. 'Over.'

The radio went silent for a moment.

'Thank you for letting me know. Over.'

Luca sighed. 'This is such poor timing, but we really need to get that message out to Alec.'

'It can't be done without official permission. That could take several hours what with everything else going on. Over.'

'Alec sent you a message to evacuate. He sent the warning hours ago. He is our best hope.'

Debs' brother paused. 'I will do all I can. What is the message? Over.'

'Firstly, tell him that Willow and Luca have sent the message and are at ground level three. Then that he needs to find and show the video message that Eban sent from Outside. It needs to be the original version. Did you get that?'

'Willow and Luca send this message. Find and show original video message from Outside,' he confirmed. 'Keep the tapper on this channel. Over.'

'All correct. Thanks. Over.'

'Excellent. And good luck. Over and out.'

Willow propped herself up in the chair. 'That was easy enough. I didn't know that anyone had warned us about the attack, let alone Alec.'

'It all happened much quicker than expected,' Luca said. 'The Emundabit timer was overridden by the person who wants everything destroyed.'

Willow nodded. 'I need to get going but I think you should stay here, since those guards are still looking for you. You still have a couple of tasers?' Eban pointed to a few that were left. 'Wait here,' she said. 'I'll make sure someone comes to find you when this is all over.' She beckoned Luca to her, pulled him down and kissed his cheek.

'Stay safe, mum,' Luca said quietly.

'I have no intention of doing that!' Willow said as she turned her chair around. 'It has taken years but now I'm ready for this fight.' Eban opened the door as Luca began to re-organise the cardboard sheets, not wanting to watch his mother disappear again. He hoped that the Tropolite guards would think her harmless when she returned.

Luca turned off his torch, aware that there was light coming from the main church building.

'So beautiful!' Mercy sang.

Luca turned. Everyone had left the bell tower room after his mother. He peered into the hall and it was flooded in stunning morning light. The fragmented windows were full of stained glass and the low morning rays were piercing the darkness. The cold room was transformed into a stunning spectrum of intense colour.

The largest window at the far end was an array of blues with what appeared to be a boat, waves and a person flying through the air. There was a crowd of happy people looking up into the sky. Luca could understand why Mercy had considered it beautiful. It made his head spin a little too.

All the other windows were hues of blue, some of which made up pictures or suggested images. There was a tree in one, birds in another and some creature that Luca had no name for racing across an open space.

But it was through the windows that guarded the entrance that filled the space with light. The sun streamed through the geometric shapes that flowed into one another. The windows were the brightest shades of yellow Luca had ever seen. There was no definite overall picture to be found in them, but an artist had carefully suggested and painted a soaring bird among some foliage and another of those flying people. Luca stared at it for a moment. The art was simplistic, but the intensity of the colour was matched by the look in this creature's face. Luca approached, never taking his gaze from the creature's eyes. He felt that the winged person was looking into him.

Luca's ears buzzed, his stomach lurched, and he vomited. He began to shake and could feel a scream scratching at his throat to get out. Pain seared across his brow and he collapsed to the floor.

Chapter 8

The sounds of their voices were muffled and distant, yet Luca could feel someone touching his shoulder. He tried to open his eyes, but they were too heavy, as if he was trying to open them in a dream. Pain dug into his stomach and he retched again.

'We need some water.'

It might have been seconds or hours later that he could feel his head being propped up and cool liquid offered to his lips. He licked at it thirstily. It dissolved the acidic aftertaste and trickled down his sore throat.

'What happened?' someone whispered.

'He was looking at those amazing windows.'

'But why did he collapse?'

'He can't be ill, can he? Not that quickly, surely.'

What had happened? Luca remembered the intense yellow and he coughed. But there had been more; the eyes of the winged creature. It reminded him of a character described in the book his mother used to read to him. It was as if it had come to life and had captured his attention. Now it had somehow seen him completely. The eyes had not looked away when all his guilt had been on display. They had looked deeper and revealed even more. Not only was Debs dead because of Luca but now his mother was going back into the library to keep her son safe and hiding what could be her invite to death. Luca wanted to turn away. He didn't want to look at it anymore, but those eyes seemed to even invade in this place, whilst he lay on the church floor. They kept their focus on him. He could not look away and he was transfixed by their depth. The deeper he looked the more he saw. It was as if flashes of his childhood, the darkest and loneliest of moments were suddenly bathed in glorious yellow sunlight, laughter and the closeness of a friend. Other moments when he was falling into despair and had gripped on to the finest of threads of hope he saw that he was, in fact, secured with the thickest of ropes that lifted him up. Those eyes were not filled with accusation but were looking at him with love.

He sighed and could feel his body relaxing at last.

'Tropolis did this to him.' Kelsee leaned close to him. 'It's alright to open your eyes. We are nowhere near the colours and safe here.'

Luca squinted at her. How did she know about the intense colours having an effect on him? They had moved him back into the tower room. He felt light headed. 'What happened?'

'I don't know for sure,' Kelsee began, 'But I think it could be left over from the prize.'

Luca lifted his head and searched for the water again. He took a gulp.

'Slowly!' Kelsee said.

'The prize?' Luca asked.

'I've seen it before. Do you remember the Connections Test?' Kelsee fiddled with her fingers. 'Of course you'll remember the Connections Test. Well, your one wasn't shown on the Network was it?'

Luca had wanted to forget the Connections Test. It had been a disorientating test of the mind that measured how the constants thought.

'The cameras failed,' Luca said flatly remembering the mess he had made during the test and how relieved he had been spared the embarrassment.

'That's what they said, but I'm beginning to think that not everything they say can be trusted. They didn't want us to see it.' Kelsee shook her head. 'But it was the coloured boxes at the end wasn't it.' Kelsee frowned. 'What happened?'

Luca sighed and bit down on his lip before he answered. 'I opened them all.' His vision began to swim in and out of focus. He laid down again.

'I know what they did. They tried to catch him and what's the term ... brainwash him, to conform him. The Connections Test is all about the contestants' ability to become part of Tropolite life. If the simulations prove that the contestant is too far removed, the Prize judges intervene. They make the contestants what they want.'

'How do you know that?'

'I've seen enough Compassion Prize contestants changed after that particular test. Their characters are altered somehow, they are different on screen.'

'The pill!' Mercy said. 'They gave him and me a pill at the end of the test. I didn't take it, but Luca did.'

'Only half,' Luca said. 'Alec didn't want me to take it. He kept shaking his head. When I spat it out, he stamped on it.'

Kelsee glanced towards the door. 'Those windows are yellow. What was in the yellow box?'

Luca shook his head. 'How do you know this?'

Kelsee waited. 'What was it?'

'You don't want to know,' Luca replied, covering his eyes.

'Alright.' Kelsee stroked his hair. 'What you just felt – now, was that the same as when you looked in the yellow box?'

'To start with it felt like all the boxes mixed together.' Luca glanced at them all. They were watching him closely.

'How are you feeling now mate?' Eban asked passing him the water again.

'Has it happened before?' Kelsee asked, not distracted by Eban's question.

Luca nodded. But he never made the connection with the test. 'It's just so stupid.' He sat up and took another gulp of water and his vision steadied.

Kelsee disagreed. 'It isn't your fault.' She paused. 'But it was such a massive reaction. I'm not sure how to help. I guess, make sure you stay away from colours.'

'Tropolis would be ideal then since they don't like colour.' Luca swirled the water in cup.

Kelsee laughed a little. 'There might be more to that than you think.'

'But I don't think it will happen again,' Luca added.

Mercy tilted her head.

Luca sighed. 'Yellow, and I guess all those colours, had been forced to represent all sorts of stuff to me, they made me feel at odds with what was actually happening. I knew it, I felt it. There was sudden fear or anxiety, so overwhelming that they really didn't fit.' The others looked confused. 'What matters is the prize judges got it wrong. They don't know who I am, and they can't tell me what to feel. I think their pill and their power just got broken.'

Mercy smiled. 'We know who you are.'

Luca wanted to avoid her gaze. She had spoken so kindly and with so much affection that he didn't deserve. He knew he needed to meet her face to face. 'I left the curtain drawn at the house. They found the gear because I let them see the lights when no one was in.' He turned to Eban. 'It is my fault that all your hard work is wasted and all the gear, gone. If I had closed the curtain, Debs would be alive, the video would have been broadcast and Outside, along with Campion, would be in Tropolis right now.'

Eban raised his palms. 'Woah!' He barked a laugh. 'You mate, need to ease up on yourself!'

'It is my fault,' Luca stated.

'I was not getting into the Network,' Eban replied. 'You could say it was my fault.'

Mercy shook her head. 'No, it was my fault for breaking the screen on the laptop.'

Kelsee nodded. 'True. But you could also say that everything is my fault because I'm related to the man who created the Compassion Prize.'

'Stop it.' Luca reached out to Kelsee. He looked at all his friends. 'Stop it all of you. You aren't to blame.'

Mercy held his gaze. 'And neither are you.' Luca's breath caught and his eyes prickled. He bit down on his lip. 'What has happened is not your responsibility, stop claiming it.'

Mercy was right, of course. The truth carried a weighty lightness.

'I'm sorry I left the curtain open,' Luca said quietly.

'I'm sorry I broke the laptop.'

'I'm sorry that the Compassion Prize was ever started.'

'And I'm sorry I haven't got to that video ...' Eban winked at them. 'Well, not yet anyway!' The tension was broken, and everyone laughed. 'I have some new ideas now though.'

Suddenly the tapper came to life.

'Ground level three, this is the tower. Come in. Over.'

Luca pulled out the tapper and depressed it. 'This is ground level three. Over.'

'I have a message for you.'

Chapter 9

Luca grinned widely.

'I may not have gone through all the protocols but as command just isn't available right now, I've just gone straight ahead. Your friend Alec was easy to reach when you know where to look. He has said to go to a Maglev station that is fairly nearby ground level three. He'll meet you there at midday. To get to the station you'll need to head north out of the village. If you keep to the road ... no wait, there are quite a few junctions.' He was silent for a moment. 'If you keep on a north easterly direction you should be alright. The signposts were removed years ago. I'm sorry I can't be more help. Over.'

Kelsee let out a disgusted snort but Luca would not let his spirits be lowered.

'There are maps in that folder. Get them out.' He hurried Kelsee along. 'Message received. North east, confirmed. Thank you tower. Please wait a moment – er, stand by.'

Luca shuffled through the paper and pulled out the map with crosses on it. He took the tapper. 'Tower? Does the station have a grid reference? Over.'

Captain Debs brother read them out slowly and repeated himself three times before the friends had found the location.

Luca traced the winding road and could see the junctions that the tower had mentioned and a marked cross at the location of ground level three. 'Copy that, Tower. Thanks. We have the location on a map. Over.'

'Great, keep in touch. Over.'

'Tower? Are Campion and the Outsiders in Tropolis yet? Over.'

'There has been no movement on that front. I do know that the Outsider community have come into their own though, and they got safely through the night. How is the situation there? Over.'

'I'm hoping that you will be hearing good news soon.' Luca said smiling at his friends. 'Ground level three will be fighting back. Over'

'Copy that. I'll look forward to that report. Over. Out.'

Luca got to his feet. 'If we're to meet Alec at midday, we need to go now.'

'But Willow said to wait here,' Kelsee said half smiling.

'Alec can get into the media suite and access that video,' Eban stated. 'We need to get all the information we have to him.'

There was very little to gather up. Kelsee secured all the papers, rolled them and tucked them into her pocket. Eban checked that the tasers that they had kept back were safely stowed away. He even added a few batteries and extra gas cylinders to his pockets. Luca flicked through the channels on the radio clipped at his waist. There were still no voices.

Kelsee cautiously opened the door to the main church building. She peered at Luca.

He stepped into the room, which was still ablaze with golden light and felt nothing but amazement at the beauty. He giggled a little before he pulled on the heavy front door. It scraped on the flagstones, just like it had done for many years, wearing a smooth groove, but the sound that echoed was not as empty as Luca had remembered it – things were different, there was hope.

The church was close to the edge of the village, but the friends still moved with caution. They kept to the shadows and barely spoke until they had reached the last of the dwellings. There had been movement in the house near to Alard's burnt out home. Luca wished that they could rescue something that might help Eban, but the meeting with Alec would be enough, there would be no need to put themselves in danger.

Luca was grateful that this road was surrounded with high hedges to guard their way. Occasionally, there would be a break in the hedgerow because of a wide gate or a tumble-down tree. These gaps offered stunning views across wild fields where the warmth of the sun caused mist to rise and curl across the landscape like gentle waves ready and inviting to swim in.

The overnight rain had left the potholed road flooded with puddles and a stream of water running off the fields and along the gutters. Sparkles from raindrops captured on spiders' webs twinkled in the sunlight. The sky was bright and almost cloud free, but the chill caused Luca's breath to appear like smoke in the air.

Mercy referred to the map several times, guiding them towards the rendezvous. She walked ahead with Eban.

Kelsee was tiring. Luca offered his hand and she took it willingly, leaning into his arm and snuggling closer. She laughed when she heard Luca's stomach growling loudly.

She sighed and rubbed her temple. Luca peered at her. She was frowning.

'You alright?'

'Headache. I think it's just a headache.' She tried to reassure him with a smile. 'Probably just a bit hungry.'

Luca pulled her closer and wrapped his arm around her waist. He dipped his lips to her head and kissed her. 'Sorry I can't help with that.'

He quickly scanned the hedgerow for berries, hoping that he might find some of the dark juicy morsels that Alec had eaten before the Endurance Test, but it seemed their season was short lived. Luca saw the branches of a tree laden with golden fruit ahead.

'Are they edible?' he asked.

Kelsee laughed louder and nodded. 'They're apples.'

When they approached, the ground was littered with spoilt and bruised apples. Luca jumped up and gripped the branch, his weight causing it to bend. Kelsee plucked four of the largest apples, called to Eban and Mercy and handed them out.

'This is the best apple I've ever tasted!' Kelsee said.

'Me too!' laughed Luca.

Kelsee wagged her finger at him. 'It's the only apple you've ever tasted isn't it?'

The sun's rays were now spilling over the hedges and onto the road. The warmth it provided was very welcome. Luca lifted his face to the light and closed his eyes.

A gentle but consistent buzzing distracted him. He squinted into the sun and a triplet of Tropolite drones flew overhead.

'Hide!' he urged.

Luca pushed his friends out of the road and tucked himself against the bushes, hiding from view. Luca's heart beat hard and fast. The drones flew overhead and ignored them. They were not following the road but flying due south towards the sea.

He pulled out the tapper and pressed the button. 'Tower? Come in Tower!'

'This is the tower. Over.'

'Ground level three reporting. Tropolite drones heading your way from the north. Three of them. You need to get out of there, over.'

'Repeat please, over.'

'Tropolis is going to attack. Three drones are coming your way. Over.'

'Message received and understood.' The sound of a claxon buzzed through the speaker on the tapper. 'Thanks for the warning. Over. Out.'

Luca could feel the warmth draining out of him. He searched for the Emundabit cube in his pocket. He dreaded pulling it out for fear that the threat had been reawakened. He opened his hand slowly. The cube sat lightless on the palm of his hand.

'It's not been reset,' Eban said.

'But that only means one thing,' Luca replied. 'Hutchings is in Tropolis and she knows what we did.'

Chapter 10

The urgency to get to the Maglev station seemed greater than ever. Hutchings had to be stopped.

Luca ran his hand through his hair as he considered just how dangerous she might be. Her plan for Emundabit had failed, but now she might be feeling cornered; even a small rat could fight like a fox when it was threatened. Luca knew that those who would be saved in the ark would be the ones she had chosen – they were her allies or at least the ones she needed to succeed and everyone else was surplus. Everyone else would be in danger. She had already sent the Tropolites out to fight her battle with Campion and Outside. She had used them as a shield around herself. Luca couldn't bring himself to justify her logic or her attitude to others. Her power had to be demolished. He tried to take his thoughts away from the disgust and steer them towards a solution, an answer to her destruction of those around her. What were her flaws? The only brightness in his thinking was that she had wanted to conceal her involvement all along. She had hidden behind Harland Barret so that he would take any blame or retaliation. As long as she wouldn't come out into the open, they had a chance to create her biggest fear; exposure. Luca knew that the video would be the best way to expose what she had intended for the people of Outside. He hoped that the Tropolites would respond in the same way that Kelsee had; shock and realisation. But there was more to her. She had gently pushed the boundaries until Tropolis was so far removed from what was healthy. She was a patient woman, she would not be rushed. Luca knew she enjoyed the planning and manipulation, since he had witnessed that first hand at the mansion. If they could force her hand, maybe she would make mistakes. The drones and attacks were part of the Emundabit plan. She would carry out the details of that plan, one by one unless they stopped her or forced her to act otherwise.

Luca pulled out the map again. He could hear his heartbeat thudding in his ears and his hands were trembling.

'Do you think they'll be alright?' Kelsee asked.

Eban shrugged. 'They missed the target last time, perhaps they will do so again.'

Luca pointed to the map. 'I don't think we'll get to the station in time.' He peered up. Mercy was rubbing her chin. 'We need to meet Alec,' Luca argued. 'We can't mess this up.' He traced his finger along the road route as it arched a wide semicircle to the station. 'We can follow that,' Luca began, 'But in the space between here and there is this wide stretch of land.' He jabbed his finger at the spot. 'There are all these other paths through that patch.'

'The tower said to take the road,' Mercy said.

'The tower didn't know we had a map we could read.' Luca replied. 'They wouldn't give us directions through that lot, it would be far too complicated. But with a map, we can do it.'

Mercy turned to Eban.

'It will be quicker.' Luca said, determined he was right.

'I say we try,' Kelsee said nodding.

Eban looked at the map. 'It's not very clear print.'

'Yes but,' Luca said, 'the route is fairly easy, there are a few changes of path but even if we generally stayed walking in the same direction we should be able meet the road further up.'

Eban shrugged. 'It might save us some time.'

'And we wouldn't be noticed by the drones.'

'The drones aren't flown by people,' Kelsee said matter of factly, 'They are operated remotely.' Luca frowned at her. 'Oh, but I expect they have cameras or something.'

'We should stay safe,' Mercy said. 'We need to get our message to Alec.'

Luca sighed. 'This will be safe.'

Just before the next junction, the hedges gave way to a tall, rusty chain link fence. Luca approached and peered through. He couldn't see far as there was a steep bank that rose high on the other side.

'We need to get to the other side, over there.' He looked up. The fence was too high to climb. They followed it a little further on and found that a low-down section appeared to have rusted through and had sprung loose.

As Luca pulled at the wires, weeds that had used the fence as support were uprooted. The fence rattled and vibrated with his effort. He lifted the loose section out of the way so that the others could duck through.

The others waited for Luca to join them. The incline, created by large slabs of concrete, was covered with rambling but weak looking plants that had grown out of the cracks in a messy lattice.

'There should be a path just the other side.'

They clambered up the bank, their feet slipping on the wet leaves and debris and their clothes catching on the brambles. At the top Luca stood wide eyed at the view. There was also an abundance of trees, oddly shaped and out of place rocks and a twisting metal structure in the distance that undulated with extreme gradients. It was so unfamiliar that Luca turned back to the fence and bit down on his lip, a moment of hesitation niggling him. A flash of light caught his attention far in the distance. He looked away. He knew that this new route would be quicker.

Luca focused on the possibility. The bank sloped down on this side and there was a path at the foot of it; the path had been in the exact place that he had said it would be. He paused. The others looked at him, questioning his every move, sceptical of the plan.

A rumbling bang filtered through the air from behind them. The drones must have hit a mark. They had to keep moving.

Luca carefully jogged down the bank and onto the trail.

'This way,' he said confidently.

The track was strewn with dead leaves and fallen branches. Short iron railings lined the path and a couple of benches crouched under a large tree. Opposite them was a still river, covered in thick green weed, that snaked away into a cave. The route followed the rocky outcrop until it reached a bridge which arched over the water and led away. Luca peered down from the bridge. A strange, hollow creature was fixed to the side of the river. Luca edged closer. Just behind it was a mossy flood lamp.

Eban reached out to the rock. He ran his hand over its surface and then knocked on it. A low hollow sound came back.

'None of this is real!'

Luca looked further up the stagnant river and saw a log shaped boat with a bright red seating strip in its hollowed out interior. The weeds had grown tall and prevented it from floating further down the water channel.

They crossed the bridge and noticed more signs of the people who had once used this place. There was a cabin just around the corner with a counter, broken shelves and half a sign that hung from one chain. Along the path there were also street lamps and litter bins, now covered with a layer of grime and various plant life. This place didn't just have an air of abandonment, but of having been ransacked for anything useful. The cabin had runners for a metal shutter, but the shutter was long gone, and the chairs that would have been useful to sit at for the tables had been taken too. Luca wondered if Campion had been here. Perhaps they had taken all the resources they could carry. That could explain the gap in the fence.

The friends passed a covered circular raised platform with plastic animals tipped to one side.

'A carousel!' Kelsee said. 'How sad that they have destroyed it.' She reached for Luca's hand. 'My grandfather told me all about these. He showed me pictures of when he was a little boy with his family. He was sat on a horse.' Luca shrugged. 'You would sit on the horses and then they would go up and down as the carousel span round.' She sighed. 'I don't know where it was ... perhaps it was here.'

'This place has been abandoned for years.'

'I don't like it here,' Mercy said. 'Let's get to the road.'

The paths in the park curled and twisted back on themselves. Luca did his best but after a few minutes of walking they were back at the carousel.

'Oh!' Kelsee exclaimed. 'I think ...'

'I know!' Luca said irritated. 'This map is useless. It doesn't have all the paths on it.'

'We could always go back to the road,' Mercy suggested.

'Or we could keep heading towards that roller coaster,' Kelsee said pointing to the metal track that was higher than the trees.

Luca had no idea what a roller coaster was but was happy for the support. He nodded and marched off along the path.

It was easier when there was something to focus on. Luca was grateful that the trees had lost many of their leaves and he could keep catching glimpses of the twisting framework. Mercy walked close to Eban and Luca could understand why. It might have been daylight but at almost every turn there was a creature, statue or something moulded in plastic to create a scare. Luca jumped when a large mouth with sharp fangs formed the doorway into another section of the park.

Kelsee did her best to describe what this place could have been once. If it had been as busy as she described, if there had been people here with smiles on their faces and music playing, perhaps the scenery would have entertained or at least made sense in some way. But this place was deserted, and the leering faces of the statues were unnerving. Their features were half obscured by ivy and trails of dirt and mildew dulled their bright colours. It was the neglect and abandonment that reminded Luca of his beginnings. He may have felt at home in a place like this a few weeks before, but it was different now. He had been changed, not so much by the Prize, but by the people that now surrounded him. They had given him a reason to step out and accepted him when he had done so. Mercy and Eban had been the ones who had guided him, but it seemed more than that. They had, it seemed, put even more faith in him at this moment. They showed him that they were confident in his plans and his voice, they were going along with his crazy idea to navigate this park and all to stop Hutchings. Luca bit down on his lip. What if he was wrong? What if his voice wasn't strong enough for Tropolis to hear? What if no one else would listen?

Luca tried to distract himself. He made an attempt to contact the tower on the tapper, but even this seemed to be doomed for failure as the only sounds that he heard in reply were crackles. He wondered if the flash had been one of the sea forts. He was certain that the headquarters must have been much further away, but he had no way of really knowing. He tried again to contact them and when he had no reply he gave the message anyway in the hope that someone would hear. He expressed his longing that they were safe.

Kelsee tucked her arm in his as he dug his hands deep into his pockets. She leaned in close, but he felt very little comfort.

Luca was grateful for the distraction of the skeletal metal frame as twisted and turned above them and around them. There was a carriage at the platform and another stopped just before it reached the pinnacle of the uphill section.

'It looks like the Maglev rail went a bit wrong!' Eban laughed.

They had got to the roller coaster track, but Luca could only guess the direction from here. 'I think we should keep going this way. Anyone else have any ideas?'

'Seems logical,' Eban replied. 'I guess if we keep the track behind us we will still be heading in the same direction.'

Luca agreed.

'Let's keep moving,' Mercy urged.

There were several other very large structures with metal tracks and bolted frames. Since some of the buildings had no roof, again, Luca wondered if Campion had gleaned the metal sheeting parts in particular. There were larger cabins near to these structures with doors that had been pushed open or broken in some way. When Luca peered inside, they were virtually empty except for the piles of leaves that had blown in and had settled on broken and possibly useless items. Luca knew that they would still have credit value if they had been found in Outside.

'Eban!' Kelsee cried. 'There are security cameras in this one. Can you use them?'

Eban rushed in. He shook his head. On closer inspection, the wires had been pulled out of the cameras and the walls. 'Everywhere has already been stripped.'

Luca pulled on Eban's sleeve. 'We don't have time for this.'

Mercy had walked on ahead. 'Luca!' Mercy called excitedly. They all ran to catch up. 'We've done it!' A large sign stretched across the wide pathway. 'Thank you for visiting. Come again soon!'

The turnstiles turned easily and Luca was momentarily taken back to Outside, only here you didn't need your chip to unlock the gate and access the other world.

The sun was nearing its highest point. They hurried.

They were soon in an open tarmacked area with flaky fading white rectangular markings. There were a few trees dotted here and there with regimented lampposts in a gridded design. Large painted arrows marked the exit.

Mercy's tension was gone, and she was being more assertive again. She took the lead with Eban and Kelsee behind her.

They had almost reached the centre of the tarmac when a buzzing sound made Luca shiver.

'Run!' he yelled. 'Drones!'

Mercy and Eban ran on ahead but Kelsee collapsed to the ground. She had not tripped or fallen but was huddled in a ball holding her head between her knees. Luca tried to pull her to her feet.

'Come on!'

Kelsee resisted and seemed to regress deeper.

Luca tucked his hand under her knees and the other under her arm. He strained to lift her.

It was as if the sudden touch had woken her a little and she wrapped her arms around Luca's neck hiding her face from the world.

Luca struggled to stand, but once he was back on his feet, he stumbled as fast as he could to the cover of trees at the far side. Eban turned and began to run towards Luca.

'No!' Luca shouted. 'Hide!'

Both Mercy and Eban sprinted towards the other side but before they were near to cover a formation of drones flew overhead. Luca peered up. They were much higher than the triplet had been, but this group numbered at least a dozen. Luca watched them as they passed over. In his mind he was wishing them too high to notice them and too busy to return. Kelsee gripped Luca with even more determination and buried her face into his coat.

It seemed that his wish had come true. The drones vanished just as quickly as they had appeared.

Luca lowered Kelsee when he got to the shade of the trees. She was shaky on her feet but refused to use Luca's offered hand to balance herself.

'What happened? Are you alright?'

Kelsee swallowed hard but just nodded.

'Do you think they saw us? Luca asked Eban and Mercy.

'I don't know,' Mercy said, 'But they were obviously sent out on a mission more important than to pick us out.'

Kelsee had stopped stumbling about and was now steady on her feet again.

'Do you think you can walk?' asked Luca. Kelsee nodded but did not look Luca in the face. Her cheeks were flushed, and Luca didn't want to embarrass her further. 'Then we should keep moving.' He reached over to Kelsee, took her hand and threaded her arm through his. 'You can lean on me,' he said quietly in her ear.

At the edge of the trees were two massive silver palisade gates. They weren't as ornate as the Compassion gate in Outside, but appeared to be made from the same metal. There were no rust marks to the prongs, but creeping plants had grown from either side and were now so established that the metal rungs at either edge were twisted and bent under pressure from the growth. The last remaining red leaves clung to the plant, but a bed of discarded beauty had been left at the foot of the gates. At the centre, where the gates met, there was a rusted chain and padlock.

Eban waded through fiery coloured leaves and pulled at the chain. He then tried to push at the gates to see if they would open enough to squeeze through. Neither worked.

Luca fiddled with Kelsee's cold fingers and sighed. He should have stayed on the road. Now they would waste more of the precious time retracing their steps.

Eban looked up at the gates and then back at the others. He began to climb the network of branches that had woven their way through the bars.

'It's not that hard!' he called. 'Come on.'

Mercy kicked the leaves aside and clambered up behind Eban. She made it look easy.

Luca turned to Kelsee. 'Do you think you ...' But Kelsee had already let go of his arm and was following the others.

Luca rushed to join them. The branches provided numerous grips and foot holds. The growth at the very top of the gates was the hardest to navigate with branches that sprung out at odd angles, unrestrained by the metalwork. Luca was grateful for them, however, because they allowed the friends to avoid the nasty spikes that had been there to prevent intruders. The gates trembled a little with the companions' movement and at the pinnacle, when Luca had to look down, he could sense the familiar swaying being amplified by his own disorientation. He took a steadying breath, paused and allowed the sensation to pass. Once he had crossed to the other side and had something to lean against it was as if nothing had occurred.

Both Eban and Mercy had jumped the final distance, challenging each other to the height that they thought the other would avoid. They both leapt, laughing a little at their game. Kelsee lowered herself quietly to the lowest branches and didn't take part. Luca did the same.

'Where to now?' Eban asked.

Luca opened the folded map and pointed right. 'That way, then the first left.'

Kelsee came close to Luca and shivered. He wrapped his arm around her and they walked together. It was comforting to be back on the high hedged roads again. Luca breathed more easily. He was relieved that his plan to cut through the park hadn't cost them more time after all and that Eban had been willing and able to show them a way out. Luca peered at Kelsee. Her lack of chatter was unnerving. He rubbed her arm and tried to make her feel better, but it made very little difference to her demeanour.

Houses began to interrupt the countryside as they sat nestled behind hedgerows and trees that overhung the road. These buildings were roofless or broken down in some way. Some of them had no doors or broken windows and all of them had overflowing gardens. Soon the friends were passing whole streets, yet it appeared that many of these structures had been damaged purposefully and violently. Where whole houses had once stood there were just a few tumble-down walls, chimney stacks left and the concrete footprints of the foundations piled high with rubble.

Luca thought of the Campion settlement. Campion had been fortunate to find a village relatively untouched over time. Perhaps they had searched for a place to house their people and ground level three had been the only place left standing. Luca shook his head. If there was a ground level three, that must mean that there were other communities at level one and two, he even entertained the thought that perhaps there were communities all over the countryside surviving away from Tropolis but linked together and supporting one another. These small communities could have gone unnoticed by Tropolis for decades. Luca took a deep breath. They might have still been living in obscurity if it hadn't had been for Mercy, Eban and himself. He could feel the strength of that responsibility squeeze his lungs and lower his gaze. He gently exhaled. Hutchings would have released Emundabit at some point, as her plan was not determined by Luca's existence. He straightened his shoulders and didn't allow the accusation to find a landing point in his heart. Luca may not have set this in motion, but he was resolute that he would do all that he could to stop it.

He pulled out the tapper from his pocket and twisted it to the channel that he had been able to speak with Debs on. He hoped that he would hear of ground level three being freed, but the tapper was silent. He dared not try to communicate with them. He would have to be patient and wait it out.

They continued to walk through the broken town. Luca was beginning to wonder if this place would have a station when they came to a level crossing. The road was raised at either side of the rail but was damaged and crumbling away. He peered down the track both ways and there was no sign of a Maglev.

'We've found the station!' Mercy said pointing to the raised platform to one side.

Luca viewed the track. Both ways were clear from weeds and the trees that had grown were trimmed, or at least grew in such a way that a Maglev could pass. These little signals indicated that this may have been a place that the Maglev might have used almost regularly.

'Are we in time?' Luca asked.

Eban shrugged and looked up into the sky. 'I hope so. Check with the tower.'

Luca radioed through and they had arrived with ten minutes to spare. Luca was grateful once again, that Eban had found a way over the gates.

There was very little direct sunlight on the platform. A deep shelter stretched from the brick building to the edge of the platform. There was only one rickety bench that sat far enough up the platform to be bathed in the sunlight, but it was not strong enough to sit on. The timber was rotten and the metal struts were corroded into orange flaky layers. The friends chose to sit huddled against the wall instead.

Luca's feet ached and his legs were sore from all the walking. There was a slight twinge of pain where he had stretched a little too far when climbing the gate, but it was the silence of the station that concerned him the most. He had rushed everyone to get them here and now they were just waiting. The chill of the morning had never lifted from the station, and now, perched on the cold concrete, Luca experienced it seeping into his body.

Kelsee had taken to curling herself up with only her eyes peeking out between the tops of her knees and the hood of her jacket. She wrapped her arms tightly around her legs and barely moved. Eban could not sit still, within a moment he was up and pacing the platform, peering into windows and trying the doors for any that were unlocked. Mercy watched all that was going on. She smiled at Eban's impatience and frowned at Luca, twitching her chin towards him and then eying Kelsee. After a few attempts, she finally asked Kelsee if she was alright. Kelsee nodded quickly but remained silent.

Luca had been oblivious to Mercy's concern but now, since she had also noticed Kelsee's unusual silence, he began to worry more. He rubbed his neck and sat closer to her. He put his arm around her and she jumped, finally making eye contact with him. She looked away quickly and shifted in such a way that Luca pulled away, not welcome or wanted.

'It's here!' Eban said leaning back from the platform edge.

There was a very faint rumble and a slight vibration. Luca helped Mercy to her feet and turned to offer Kelsee his hand, but she had already stood up.

A single, sleek and polished carriage hurried to the station and then slowed. It halted without a jolt. Luca tried to peek into the window, but the curved sides reflected the sunlight. Kelsee punched the button on the side of the train and the door lifted out towards them with a hushing sound and then slid up over the roof.

'Alec!' Luca cried out. 'Alec?' But the train was empty.

Chapter 11

Luca jumped on board and searched the carriage, half expecting to find Alec unconscious on the floor. He pulled off a note taped to the control panel. On it was scrawled a seven-digit code.

Mercy and Eban peered in.

'Now what?' Luca said. 'Do you think Alec got caught?'

Mercy puffed out a breath. 'I don't know.'

'It must be midday,' Mercy reasoned. 'He should be here.'

'Hutchings wanted him dead.' Luca was wide eyed. 'She is in Tropolis now.'

'Maybe that is why he isn't here,' Eban said. 'He's keeping his distance.'

'Or she already has him,' Kelsee whispered.

Luca glanced at Kelsee. She had barely said anything, and this was not what he wanted to hear. 'What if Campion never got that warning about the Emundabit attack? What if Hutchings has him now?'

'Alec is a shrewd man,' Eban said confidently. 'He has been working with Campion for a long time and I think he would know where to go if he needed to escape.'

Luca hoped Eban was right. 'Maybe this was the best he could do.'

'Do you think we should get in?' Kelsee asked. 'It could be a trap.'

'It might be,' Luca replied. 'But we don't have much choice. We need to get that message out to the Tropolite people. If we need to help Alec or do it ourselves, either way, we can't do that from here.'

'What's that?' Mercy asked looking at the tab of paper.

'I think it is a destination code.' Luca turned to Kelsee. 'Do you know this 600 6058?'

Kelsee looked at it. 'The first three digits are for the Tropolis centre, I don't know what station it is for though.'

Luca watched her closely. Her voice was strained and empty of emotion. She glanced up at him and smiled, although it didn't reflect any happiness in her eyes.

'Can we stop the Maglev once we are on it or do we need another code?' Eban asked.

Kelsee rubbed her forehead and took a sharp breath. 'Once you are on the train you can stop at any of the stations on the route you have chosen. If you get off, however, the train will continue the journey without you to its pre-programmed destination. It will only leave that final destination if a new code is given or if summoned by the control centre.'

'But can a Maglev be stopped from a station on the route?' Luca asked.

'No,' Kelsee said. 'They are automatic, driverless trains.' She wandered over to the Maglev, pushed past Luca and climbed inside. 'They will only stop at pre-programmed places or from a person able to change the code from either inside the train or the control centre. You can't make a Maglev stop from a station. You only have one destination, so this Maglev can only be accessed from that station because that is where it terminates.'

'If that is the case,' Luca began, 'We can use this Maglev to get us into Tropolis or at least nearer to it – we can just add a different code. We don't have to go to the final destination. He moved into the carriage, and so did the others. 'It's warmer in here and much quicker than walking.'

The swish of the door closed behind them, but the Maglev remained still awaiting the next instruction.

The chill was quickly locked on the other side. The warm carriage was not as luxurious as Harland's Maglev train, but there was still a small selection of food in a modest chiller cabinet. Kelsee automatically pulled out a couple of packets, placed them onto plates and put them into the oven to heat. As soon as the oven bleeped she placed two more meals inside.

'Should we program the journey?' Luca asked crumpling the paper in his hand. 'I think we should have a plan or something.'

'I don't think we should go to that destination,' Mercy said.

'We need to get to Alec or the media suite,' Eban said. 'That's enough of a plan for now.' He had opened the packet of steaming food. 'It's going to take some time to get there, the sooner we leave, the sooner we stop the drones, the sooner we can try to make a difference.'

Luca opened the control panel. 'What about another code?' Luca looked at Kelsee. 'Do you know the code for the station under the contestants' building?

Kelsee shook her head.

'That probably wouldn't be a good idea,' Eban said. 'We don't want to end up crashing at the tunnel if the Maglev takes us that way.'

Luca remembered the crumpled Maglev at the tunnel and didn't want to end up there. He was uneasy, but he tapped in the code that had been provided since it would most likely be a crash free route. The train began to move back up the track. The screen showed a list of similar codes in a dim font but with their code highligted in red at the very bottom. Luca breathed a little easier. There was a way of knowing if they were approaching the unknown destination and stopping the Maglev.

The hot food was just what they needed, but having full stomachs made them all a little sleepy. Luca refused to get too comfy. A thousand different scenarios played out in his mind about what had happened to Alec and what he would find in Tropolis. The more he allowed those thoughts to develop the tighter the muscles in his shoulders and back became. Mercy, who had been watching the world flash by the window, suddenly turned to Luca.

'You'll waste too much energy worrying about what hasn't even happened.' She smiled gently.

'You don't know what's happened,' Luca replied dully.

Mercy nodded in agreement, 'But I'd prefer to think of the good.'

'Nothing good has come out of Tropolis.'

'That's not fair or true,' Mercy said. She pointed to Kelsee who had curled up on one of the chairs with her head resting on her folded jacket. 'You need to look beyond the whole thing and see the individuals. Kelsee is one of them; your dad is another.'

Luca swallowed a mouthful of drink and then screwed the lid back on the bottle tightly. 'But Tropolis, the power of Tropolis,' he corrected, 'has ruined any good that there could be.'

'Well think on this then,' Mercy gestured to each of them. 'Tropolis may not be good right now, but we haven't got there, and we haven't finished yet.'

Luca wanted to reply, to tell Mercy that she was somehow delusional for thinking so highly of what she could do, of what they could do, but he found himself daring to believe her. What they had planned could change life for the Tropolites. It was a relatively simple thing, to reveal the truth that the enemy was not those trying to get in, but those that had held them back for so long. The simple message to Alec and getting that video shown for what it was before it was manipulated could be the stain that everyone would see on Hutchings' white clothes.

Luca tried to breathe deeply. 'You're right,' he said quietly. He wanted to think that they would be the ones to bring goodness to

Tropolis, but he found himself suffocating under the responsibility of it. What if they failed? He started to tap the bottle on his knuckle watching the liquid swirl. 'I'm half Tropolite and half Outsider, yet I don't fit in either of those places anymore.' He leaned forward. 'I need this place to change and I hope we can do it.'

Mercy tilted her head to one side. 'I don't know what I am. I grew up in Outside, I have Campion inked in my skin and I want freedom for Tropolis. I know that feeling of not belonging yet longing for the different places to be liberated.'

Eban began to hum a familiar tune.

Luca looked at him. 'And you?' he asked.

'I think we need to stop thinking *them* and *us*. I have seen Outsiders battle with what they should be my whole life and then discover in a moment that they are about something bigger than their own world. Being part of the prize with you is just one example.' Eban laughed a little. 'Then when Mercy was bringing the people of Campion, Outside and those that had become Tropolites together,' Eban's eyes sparkled, 'It was a remarkable thing, I wish you had seen it.'

'It is possible, Luca,' Mercy said softly.

Luca began to put aside the nagging thoughts and think on what Mercy had said. *It is possible*. He had seen it before. Eban was right in stating that he had been changed, but not because of the prize, it was being with them that had made all the difference to him. If it was possible for him to step out from being an Outsider, with an Outsider mindset it might be possible for others too. His mother had managed to physically move from the library and the place she had been trapped in and go back with possible freedom. Even the rallying of the Outsider people into becoming a community was an unthinkable reality when the heat of the year had been causing the stink to rise from the heaps. Things were changing and at a rate that he could not have thought possible. Luca looked at Eban and Mercy. Things were changing because of them, they were the ones who had done all this. He hung his head.

He was just tagging along, benefitting from being with them of course, beyond anything he could have imagined, but his role was unimportant. They were the ones that would change his world.

Kelsee began to twitch in her sleep. She kicked out and screamed.

'No! I won't do it!' she shouted as she threw her arms out. 'Leave me alone!'

Luca crouched down next to her. Her eyes flew open and she gasped.

'It was only a dream,' Luca said trying to soothe her.

Kelsee began to sob. Luca leaned in to hug her, but she shoved him away.

'Do you want to talk about it?' he asked a little hurt by her response.

Kelsee shook her head.

'What is happening? I know something is going on.'

Kelsee wiped at her cheeks angrily. She pointed at Luca. 'Don't push me,' she said through gritted teeth, 'Or I'll do it.'

Mercy pulled Luca away and stood between him and Kelsee. 'It was just a dream. Not real.'

'It felt so real,' Kelsee replied closing her eyes and swallowing hard. She pinched the back of her hand and winced. She looked up at Mercy, wide eyed. 'So real.' Kelsee propped herself up and Mercy sat down next to her.

Luca tried to lean round and catch Kelsee's attention, but she had her head on Mercy's shoulder and was crying again. He resigned himself to sit back and let Mercy take over. This whole situation proved his own belief that he was unimportant and useless.

The Maglev had taken them along a seaside track. Luca looked out over the surprisingly still water, hoping that he wouldn't see any distant smoke and flames. When larger settlements began to flash past the window, Luca began to get jittery; Tropolis was becoming ever closer. He looked at the crumpled code and he was certain that the lack of anything but the numbers scribbled down was some sort of message in itself. Alec would have said more on his note and shown some affection. Luca strained to see the massive sky scrapers and gleaming city marking the horizon.

'I don't think we should wait until we get to the station,' Luca said when the buildings were coming even closer.

'Neither do I,' agreed Mercy. 'But how close shall we get?'

Kelsee was rubbing her temples and grimacing. 'I've never come to Tropolis from this side before. Sorry I can't help.'

Luca was grateful that Kelsee was at least participating in conversation again, but she still seemed distracted and distant. She had put distance between them and he wasn't sure what he had done to deserve it or what to do to gain her trust back.

'You know more than us,' Eban said putting his face to the glass. 'If you can get us to the contestants' building.'

'You can see that from here,' Kelsee replied. 'It is the only one with the bluish colour. They made it that way so that everyone would always remember to tune in.' A single building stood out in the bland white and steel skyline. She frowned and added, 'Or they made it that way so that they would remember how much better they were than Outside.'

Luca couldn't fault her reasoning. He had another opinion on why it should stand out. Maybe it was more of a reminder to those that would dare to think differently that the power of Tropolis could do anything to any life it chose. He did not speak it out but nodded at his own wisdom. Sadly, this power was linked too closely to Kelsee and his own fragile compassion for her grandfather. He let the memory of the man crash into him again, and plans of dark revenge that he had discarded began to stutter to life under the stark richness of the city. He bit his tongue and shook his head. He had a choice to give life to those plans or to kill them off. Eventually, he chose to recall the words that Harland had uttered, begging for forgiveness at the mistake and Luca was undone. How could he go into Tropolis with a deep hatred for its inhabitants and then set them free? He couldn't. He had to let his heart burn brightly with a compassion fire.

The Tropolite inhabitants had been told to arm themselves and protect their homes against the enemy. Luca had seen the fear that the Network had fed into the broadcast and was wary that Tropolis would be a dangerous place.

'If we go to the designated station, we won't know if it was a trap before it is too late.' Luca pointed to the taser at Eban's belt. 'We may be armed but I think you might have underestimated the level of defence. I think Alec doesn't want us to go there.' Mercy tilted her head. 'He just wrote a code ... no name, no message. I'm the only family he knows is still alive. If he couldn't come for us, he would have said, he knows I can read. The lack of a message is a message in itself.'

'So, we stop soon and walk through the city,' Eban suggested. Luca threw open his hands.

'We only have those two, Luca,' Mercy said. 'If this has been a trap to get us into Tropolis, the station will be ready for us. Leaving before will mean working our way to the contestants' building through the city. You need to remember that Tropolites can be spoken to. We need to hope that we might be able to do them good.'

'Alright.' Luca agreed with Mercy. 'When?'

Kelsee had reached the panel. 'Now,' she said pressing the button to interrupt the program.

A metallic female voice played over the speakers. 'Unscheduled stop.'

Luca reached forward. 'What are you doing? Can't we get closer than that?'

Kelsee pointed to the screen. 'There are only two stations between here and the potential ambush,' Kelsee replied. 'I think that is close enough.'

'She's right,' Eban said. 'We need to give ourselves a head start incase they look for us.'

She shrugged as she picked up her jacket and put it on. The document folder dropped from the inside pocket.

Luca picked it up and handed back to Kelsee whose hand was outstretched. 'We should have checked the files,' he said. 'There must be more in there other than the meeting notes about Campion.'

Mercy looked at him. 'Meeting notes?'

Luca bit his lip. In the sudden appearance of his mother at the church he hadn't told them what he had discovered. 'The leaders had found out about people living free from Tropolis. There are records from a meeting where the Tropolite committee were discussing the torture of those that tried to escape Tropolis. Information was gathered from them about contacts, routes and where they were going to go. There are layers that are even more disturbing; the people who were in that original meeting when the people living free was discussed aren't mentioned again. They disappeared.' Luca gripped the edge of the chair and approached the window. The train wasn't slowing. 'You found something too, didn't you Kelsee?'

She shook her head and squeezed her lips together.

Luca frowned. 'Are you sure?' He remembered her putting a yellowing slip of paper in her pocket.

Kelsee flattened her hair. 'No!' She patted the folder. 'Only the bit that you saw. You folded over the corner.' She rubbed at her ear. 'I've not read it yet. There have been other, more pressing things.'

'Those documents will help in whatever justice we can bring,' Eban said. 'It makes sense that Harland would have kept them safely locked away.'

Mercy nodded. 'We can hand all that information over when we need to.'

Whether Harland had saved them to protect others from knowing or to incriminate others, Luca was not entirely sure, but he was certain of what he had seen Kelsee do. He stood closer to Kelsee. 'I hope you are feeling a bit better now,' he said desperate to see what she had been so keen to hide.

Kelsee was pale. She didn't appear to be any better at all; if she hadn't been stood so strong, Luca would have assumed that she was deathly sick. Suddenly, he wondered about the fatigue.

'You look pale,' he whispered in her ear. 'Is it the fatigue?'

Kelsee leaned into him. 'The fatigue hasn't bothered me since I met Mercy. I don't think it will affect me again.' Luca looked into her eyes and there was a flicker of the Kelsee he knew. Her warm smile was fleeting but it did beam at him for a moment. Then she shut her eyes tightly. 'If only this would stop,' she said rubbing her head once again.

Luca was still confused. Kelsee was avoiding looking at him again and he was certain of what he had seen at the church. Why would she lie? What was she hiding? He walked over to the door and peered out of the window. The train began to slow a little. He smiled kindly at Kelsee and reached out his hand to her. She was hesitant but took it. He pulled her close and wrapped his arms around her in a hug; there was no warmth in her response, but Luca needed to pretend he didn't feel it. As he let her go, he scrunched at her jacket pocket. He coughed a little to cover the sound of the paper crumpling in his hand. He slipped in into his own pocket in a swift move, released her from the hug and then took her hand again.

The Maglev stopped smoothly, and the door lifted open. The station was empty.

The friends stepped off the Maglev and into the salty, chilling air. Luca shivered. With a swish of the doorway behind him, a slight rumble and the Maglev sped off towards its final destination.

A brick archway was the only way out. As Luca walked through he could see the skyscrapers in the distance. He picked out the contestants' building and knew that it would be dark by the time they would arrive. He was grateful. Perhaps the darkness would hide them.

'Stop right there!' A deep voice shouted. 'Don't move!'

Luca's arms were pulled behind him and the taser was pulled from his belt. He could hear the others protesting as they were grabbed too. Stopping the Maglev early hadn't helped them at all.

Chapter 12

Luca tried to see who his captors were but since he was being led out in front there was no way of knowing.

They were marched down a steep hill in the opposite direction to Tropolis.

'Major, we're bringing them in. Over.'

'Excellent,' said the female voice. 'Bring them to the encampment headquarters. Over and out.'

Luca strained harder to turn around. 'Quit struggling!' the man who held Luca said angrily.

'Is that Major Thomas? Are you Campion or Outsider?' Luca asked.

'I'm not at liberty to say,' the man replied, but his tone didn't hide his fluster.

Luca relaxed and even laughed a little. Their confinement was only going to be temporary and they would be free to get to Tropolis as soon as Thomas saw who her men had dragged in.

At the base of the hill was a scooped-out inlet where the sea could pool. The natural harbour was congested with vessels of varying sizes and crowded the land where an arc of small houses and stores were situated. The cliffs rose from either side of the bay and provided the view of the tiny community. The beaches at the base of the cliffs were long and narrow. The sheer cliff was contrasted with the deep curve of grassland that led into the land. The bowl-shaped landscape provided shelter for a dark and sprawling woodland.

There was an encampment tucked away under the cover of trees that was not far from the shore. The people had used the boats, fallen wood and whatever they could find to create makeshift shelters. Several dinghies had been upturned and groups of people sat in their shade. Luca was guided through the middle of the haphazard community. He saw Outsiders sat with blue clad Campion and military dressed Tropolites. It was a confusing sight. A couple of them waved at Mercy before running off. Luca knew that Campion had ferried the Outsiders to the mainland and that the Tropolite army sent to destroy the uprising were actually prize winners and contestants from past years. Eban and Mercy had recounted the story, but he had never witnessed the remarkable sight with his own eyes. Despite being held captive and being marched off to meet the Major, Luca chuckled with delight.

They were led to a low flint building with a wide porch where tables and chairs were pushed to one side. The window in the door had been broken but covered with a couple of layers of corrugated card. A bell tinkled when the door opened, and the friends were taken in.

'We found these on the returning Maglev,' the deep voiced man said as he approached the darkest corner. He was tall and muscular. He placed the tasers and Kelsee's folder on the metal table. When he stepped away Luca saw the unmistakable buzz of cropped hair.

Major Thomas looked up from her makeshift desk. She had been thrilled to see the tasers, but her disappointment when she realised who was in front of her was not disguised.   Her frustration was evident in the deep lines that furrowed her forehead. Luca tried not to smile.

'Let them go!' she said almost defeated. She turned to the muscular man. 'Didn't you recognise the girl?'

'I thought she was the one from Outside, but I was just fulfilling orders.'

The major blinked slowly and turned back to Mercy. 'I thought you were trying to get us into Tropolis. What are you doing here?'

Mercy stepped forward. 'Good afternoon Major Thomas.'

'Enough of the niceties! What are you doing here?'

'We need to get into Tropolis.'

'Don't we all!' Thomas replied sarcastically.

The tapper buzzed at Thomas' shoulder.

'Tower to Major Thomas. Over.'

The major turned away and tapped her shoulder. 'Thomas responding. It's good to have you back. Go ahead. Over.'

'One tower went down in the attack. All other towers were cloaked in time thanks to the warning. Fourteen drones in all. Failed tower was under sustained and concentrated attack from all drones. No casualties. Unmanned and dummy tower was destroyed. Over.'

Luca smiled again. That was due to his warning. He had done some good and saved some of Campion.

'Any further reports? Over.' Major Thomas asked.

Luca listened intently. Had his mother succeeded?

'Nothing ma'am. Over.'

'Let me know as soon as you know. Over. Out.' She turned back to Luca. 'I understand that you sent that warning to the tower.' She dipped her head. 'Thank you.'

Mercy changed the subject quickly. 'Why did the drones not attack you? Tropolis knows you are here.'

The Major shrugged her shoulders. 'I wonder if they want to take out our bases first. There have been several attacks on different locations. I think that the resistance we are facing here is enough to hold us back.'

'You can't think that they will ignore you much longer,' Mercy said. 'And they'll probably know that the Maglev stopped at your station.'

Major Thomas stood. 'Do you think I am stupid? I know they will come after us sooner or later but what can I do?' She raised her chin. 'I have a duty to take care of these people, but I have no hope of getting into Tropolis with you stood before me. I need to work out a new course of action since you are here and not there!' Tiny beads of sweat had formed on Thomas' brow. 'I only have boats and pieces of settlements that might house these people. We can't stay here. I don't know what other settlements that Tropolis knows of, but there must be some.' She sighed. 'Which will be reachable? Which are still hidden?'

'You can't leave,' Mercy said. 'Tropolis needs you.'

'I think Tropolis has other ideas, don't you?' Thomas beckoned a blue clad Campion soldier. 'Emergency meeting. I want squadron leaders, captains and chief boat crew here in an hour.' She then turned to the muscular man. 'Take this lot to some of their Outsider people. I'm sure they could find something useful for them to do.'

'We can be useful here,' Mercy said. 'You need to not make any rash decisions.'

'Rash decisions? I was waiting for the go ahead into the city.' Major Thomas balled her fists. 'This is the backup plan. I knew that I would need one,' she said angrily.

Mercy stepped back. Eban took her arm and began to lead her out.

'My folder,' Kelsee said. 'Can I have my folder?' She stepped forward to take it from the Major's table.

'What's this?' Thomas picked it up and opened it. Her eyes were suddenly bright. 'No, I think I'll keep this safe. Off you go.' She ushered them away without looking up from the papers she was engrossed in.

The friends were shown from the flint building and abandoned just outside. Their guard marched back up the hill towards the station while another rushed off to gather the people Thomas had commanded.

Kelsee's cheeks were flushed and her eyes were dark. Luca pulled her away from the door.

A tall man with a stubbly excuse for a beard was leaning on the corner of the building. His dark hair was tied away from his face. He strolled up to Luca and helped him move Kelsee away from Major Thomas' headquarters.

'We weren't expecting to see you.'

'We get that a lot!' said Luca in a brisk tone.

'Fielder!' Mercy caught him about his waist and hugged him.

'Now that you are here, we were wondering if you wanted something for dinner.'

'We've just eaten, thanks,' Luca replied. He looked up at Fielder and saw him wink.

'Sounds great!' said Eban laughing.

Fielder smilcd. 'This way then.'

Kelsee stood firm. Luca pulled on her arm and eventually, after she rubbed her ears, she gave in and followed.

Fielder's wide stride meant that Mercy had to jog to keep up with him. He took the group back into the shade of the trees where there were numerous tarpaulin tents and woodland shelters. A glowing fire was being kept alight by a few Outsiders who were loading the embers with a few offerings to keep it burning. There were three people sat close by.

Luca ran forward. He reached for one of the men who stood surprisingly quickly. He was still skinny, but he didn't appear so frail, even though he should in this place. The dark circles under his eyes even seemed a little lighter. 'Dad!'

'Luca!' Amil whispered. 'You are safe.' He held him out and inspected him. 'They saw you coming in.'

Amil wrapped his arms about him and hugged him again. Luca could tell that his father was phyically stronger, but he was certain that there was a new found internal strength.

'We shouldn't be here,' Luca said pulling away from the uncomfortable affection. He looked into his father's eyes. He couldn't work out if being away from Outside had brightened them or Outside being removed from his father had made the impact. Either way, Luca could hardly find the man who had been a burden for all those years.

Luca gave a quick smile and a slight shake of his head as he tried to aquaint himself with this almost stranger. For a moment, he felt like a child again in the presence of a father who wasn't broken and sickly. He raised his eyebrows as he realised that his father had come back to life after years of being lifeless. This man was the one who had been fighting alongside his mother when Luca was young. Had they both been resurrected? Luca couldn't quite believe what he saw.

'Griffin!' Mercy stepped forward and kissed him on the cheek. 'I see you still have Fielder running your errands.'

Griffin was permenantly bent over with a curved back. 'That's about right!' he laughed. 'I'm just not up to running much these days. We saw you being brought into camp.' Griffin gestured to the dark-haired woman standing by. 'I take it you'll remember ...'

'Josetta,' Mercy said nodding. 'I won't forget you.' Josetta blushed a little. Mercy turned to Luca and Kelsee. 'Griffin is, well I guess, leading the Outsider community. You didn't meet him when you were in Outside, but he has been pushing the boundaries of Outside for years. I guess the last prize just heightened his influence in the Outsider community. And Josetta came from Outside, was a contestant in the prize and has been living in Tropolis ever since. She was sent in as the force to quell the uprising. I think your uncle Alec put the Tropolite army together and sent them in.'

Luca extended his hand. Josetta smiled at the very Tropolite greeting.

Griffin patted the logs next him. 'Sit down, sit down!' he said. 'We have lots to talk about.'

The two groups began to exchange stories of how they had arrived at the edge of Tropolis. Griffin went first.

'The resistance from Tropolis had been fatal for a few members of the Outsider and Campion rescue party. You see, we had attempted to enter the city via the wide river mouth. Major Thomas had assumed that the central city area should be the initial place to assist the Tropolites. None of us objected to her reasoning and we were content to follow her leadership. However, the violence pushed the front boats back very quickly. We were shocked at the level of hatred that the Tropolites were displaying. We pulled away from the river and there have been no other fatalities since. Tropolis are very aware they were still here, on the very outskirts of their city, but there has been no advance on the encampment. There wasn't a huge population to this seaside suburb and they left in a hurry before Campion and the rest of us landed. It was only when our troops tried to move further inland into Tropolis that there was any resistance. Major Thomas has been doing what she can. She keeps the people out of danger by holding them back and has made sure that supplies from the flint café and other building have been distributed.'

Luca was interested to hear why they hadn't moved into the city.

Griffin continued. 'Thomas has sent out a few to see if there are any ways around the Tropolites, but they have all the roads into the city covered. The bay got us off the water, but we are still trapped. We don't move forward, and we get left alone.'

Josetta opened her hands. 'They have kept my group busy, but distant from the border. I think the Major is anxious not to have anything that might look like force going towards them.'

Luca nodded. 'That's not surprising. The Tropolites have been told to arm themselves. They think we are coming in to kill them. It's probably best not to give that impression.'

Griffin frowned. 'There was one weak point from what I can glean. There were security guards but not the crowds of Tropolites down at their marina.'

'Have you seen any other action? Drones?'

'No, we haven't. Makes you wonder, why don't they attack us here?'

'We've seen what the drones can do,' Eban said sadly. 'I'm certain that if they were sent, you'd have been killed.'

'They need your blood,' Kelsee said coldly. 'They won't kill you until they have literally bled you dry.'

Luca frowned. Kelsee was correct but the bluntness was not like her. 'Emundabit was the plan that was put into place. Its role was to attack those out of Tropolis control and bring them to their knees. They sent drones to the Campion settlements and communication towers out at sea. The plan is to weaken our systems but still get all they need out of us. Well maybe.' Luca shrugged. 'The automatic and systematic control system for Emundabit has been brought down but since Hutchings is now back in Tropolis, she is now working out the commands from there. They may not be quite as co-ordinated, but they are still as deadly and possibly more so.'

'Hutchings?' Griffin asked.

'Harland Barret's personal assistant,' Josetta clarified.

'Harland is dead,' Kelsee said with tears in her eyes. 'Luca, please explain.'

Luca told them about the events at the mansion, the sickly old man who had not ruled for a long time and Mara Hutchings who had taken power covertly. He pulled out the Emundabit cube and balanced it on the log in front of him as he told them how Eban had disabled the code. Luca was shocked that he had only sorrow for the old man who had died.

'Have you come from there?' asked Griffin.

Mercy shook her head. 'We have been at ground level three, a Campion settlement.' Mercy leaned forward onto her knees. 'There was some trouble. The man who came to Outside leading your friends,' Mercy said turning to Josetta.

'Atticus?' Josetta asked. 'He was locked up in the staff block before we left.'

'Well, he escaped and got to Campion,' Luca said with a hint of bitterness.

Josetta rubbed her knuckles. 'He is a strange one, that Atticus. He won the Prize the year he was taken to Tropolis, but he has been pleasing the authorities ever since. I have seen it a few times, the desperation to become completely Tropolite. Atticus was completely consumed by it. Whoever he was when he was an Outsider, is completely lost now.'

Mercy picked up the story. 'Ground level three was still being controlled by this man when we left but that was due to change.'

Luca looked at Amil and then kicked at the dead leaves at his feet. 'Willow was let out of the holding area and was taking back some tasers to turn that around.'

Amil smiled. 'That sounds like her,' he said proudly. 'Sounds like this Atticus fellow isn't that bright to let Willow go.'

Mercy and Eban looked at Luca. He peered up at them. He knew that Amil had only been told half the truth. He scratched his neck and swallowed hard. 'Atticus wouldn't have thought Willow was dangerous.' He glanced at Amil. 'Mum's back was crushed at the dockside and she has been unable to walk since. She wouldn't have been a threat to him.'

Amil's eyes sparkled with tears. 'I thought that she was dead for many years. When you told me she was alive but hadn't come for us I thought that ... I don't know what I thought; that she didn't love me the way I loved her, that she was happy to be free from Outside and from us. It just didn't fit with who I knew she was. I knew there was another reason why she didn't come back.'

Eban patted Amil's back. 'Willow is a stubborn woman!'

Amil laughed through the tears.

Eban laughed with Amil. 'She was not going to let her people in ground level three die. She is very brave indeed.'

Amil nodded and hugged Eban. 'She is,' he agreed. 'She really is. Atticus wouldn't know what to do with her if he knew her like I did! He certainly wouldn't let her out of his sight.'

Luca watched as Eban was able to say who Willow was without tainting her with what she had failed to do for so many years. Ultimately, she had put aside the good choice and made the right choice. He hoped and dreamed that she was alright.

Luca sighed. 'We were at ground level three to see if we could get the footage Eban had filmed. It was broadcast on the Network in Tropolis, but it was mashed up in such a way that the Tropolite people heard and saw it as a threat and as an invasion. Our aim was to let them see the full message, let them understand that you were coming to help them and that you should be let in for their good.' Luca stamped his feet. 'But now, Major Thomas is planning to take you all back to other Campion settlements leaving Tropolis to suffer. But she hasn't seen what Hutchings is like or what damage has already been done. If Thomas follows this through, I don't think there will be much of a future. Hutchings won't let us live and will find us.'

'But she hasn't attacked us here,' Josetta said. 'And Kelsee is right, the people need our blood for the cure.'

Luca blew out a breath. 'She knows that we aren't coming to attack but to rescue the Tropolite people. She saw the video. If we do that, she loses everything she has worked for. We have to be destroyed and she wants the people to do it. It will be easier to cover her tracks that way. If the people are the ones instigating and caught up in a war, she can safely blame them for the death that would come with it.' He stared at the glowing coals and reached for a long stick. 'She wants Campion, Outside and the unhealthy Tropolites to disappear. If we all die, and she is left with the healthy ones who are loyal to her and her ideals she has accomplished all she wants. I don't think she was content to lead in secret but has long been planning a much bigger and grand future for herself. She wants to rule. She is counting on all this mess and confusion to be the thing that burns us out. She thinks we are just tiny little embers that can be wiped out while she sits comfortably in her ark with her chosen few.' Sparks rose into the air as Luca poked the fire. They briefly flickered yellow and orange, fading into the chilled air. 'If Thomas hides us all, Hutchings will come after us knowing that now we are a threat to her. She won't wait. She has already sent out more drones to destroy Campion. I have no idea what she can do to a city of people, but if we don't engage in this fight, I am certain she will.' Luca looked around the few that had done so much already. 'We have to do something.'

He threw the stick onto the fire. A swirling cloud of hot particles flew about as the stick landed in the centre. The cooler outer layer gave way to the white heat of the established fire underneath. The bark from the stick caught light immediately and a burst of flames danced before them. Luca leaned back as the heat intensified.

Amil turned to Luca. 'You have added only a small stick, yet we see the change and feel the heat. If all it will take to change this around is a small stick, that is to show a film, I'll take you into Tropolis myself. If you can still get to that film, you can still change this for us.'

Josetta shrugged. 'That is all well and good, but we've seen the resistance Tropolis is putting up.'

'No, we haven't,' Amil replied. 'We have seen the resistance that Tropolis has put up for a huge number of us, but a few, taken in by a route that is unknown and weak is a different matter.'

'There is no such route!' Josetta said.

'But there is,' Amil answered.

Luca smiled.

'How do you know that?' Griffin asked.

'Because Luca and his friends got out.' Amil smiled widely. 'And it was the way that I got out of Tropolis.'

'Of course, the rubbish chute!' Luca exclaimed. 'It seems like it is the only the logical way in now we are that close.'

Chapter 13

'That would be perfect!' Luca said feeling suddenly energized. 'We can easily find our way to the contestants' building and the media suite from there.'

Kelsee put her hand on Luca's knee. 'But the marina has security.' She pointed at Griffin. 'He already said that.'

Luca put his hand on hers. 'There must be a way.' He turned to his father and Josetta.

'There is security,' Griffin said, 'but not the crowds and it is the crowds of armed Tropolites that we need to avoid.'

'I've never been to the marina,' Josetta admitted, 'But I can offer my services to help get you through whatever their security looks like. I'm sure there are more of us that would be keen to get this moving.'

Amil patted the air. 'Only a few. We need to appear to be not threatening.'

Griffin cleared his throat. 'We'll send in our best.' He looked at Fielder. 'I'm not up to a mission like that. I would slow them down. We'll have to get a plan of the building from you and then a task force can get in there.'

'Sorry?' said Mercy, leaning forward. 'You sounded as if we weren't going in.'

'That's right,' Griffin nodded. 'You have been through enough. If it is as simple as you say, we should be fine. In fact,' he gestured to Josetta, 'One of the Tropolite army could do it. I'll need details of those that have specific technical strengths as well as defence abilities.'

Luca clenched his fists. 'No!' he said, his face flushing with heat. 'This is ...'

'Quiet Luca,' Amil said placing his hand on his son's shoulder. 'Let Griffin take responsibility here, have a think about his idea. It will be better for you to be safe with us.'

'Safe?' Luca brushed his father away. 'No one is safe here.' Luca was suddenly reminded of his library bound mother. Was he to be held back?

Everyone started speaking at once. Mercy and Eban were just as indignant as Luca.

'Alright now. Let's calm this down,' Griffin said over the din of protest. 'I suggest we go and eat. I'm not sure that hunger isn't helping any of us right now.'

'Food is always a good idea,' Eban said, his smile returning.

'We'll meet back here just before twilight,' Griffin said. 'That should give me enough time to sort a team.' Griffin pulled Fielder close, began to urgently talk to him and hobbled away.

'Come and share my food,' Amil said standing.

Luca looked at the stick in the fire. The flames were dim and the wood charred.

'Are you coming?' Amil asked. 'All of you, my Luca's friends. Come have some food with me.'

Eban walked up to Luca and nudged him. 'Great idea,' Eban said reaching for the Emundabit cube and handing it back to him.

Luca was astonished at how agile his father had become. Living with the community had helped Amil more than the years of being hidden away with only Luca's bitterness to comfort him.

Amil had a small area on the perimeter of the main camp, under a tree thick with foliage. The ground beneath it was dry and soft with a thick layer of dead leaves.

He began to share out what he had. It was a tiny ration to begin with and Luca, having eaten a full meal on the Maglev, insisted his father eat it all. Amil then tried to hand out food to the others.

'Luca! Luca!' It was a female voice calling his name. Luca turned and there was no one there.

Amil stood rigid and stared at Luca. 'Willow!'

Luca quickly realised that the tapper was working in his pocket.

'Mum? Are you alright?'

'Luca! It worked!' Her voice was excited. 'Those idiots are gone, and Campion is free. Oh, over!'

Amil covered his mouth; tears were flowing down his cheeks.

Luca looked up at his father. 'Is anyone injured? What do you mean they're gone?'

'No one is hurt. Well, except for those orange guards. The two in uniform got away, but good riddance I say! They won't be back. Apparently, they were chased out of the village the way they came in. There wasn't any more of them heading our way, were there?'

'Not that I know of.'

'Where are you? I went back to the church and you were gone. I told you to stay put.'

'We got a message from Alec to get back into Tropolis.' The radio went silent for a while. 'Are you still there? Can you hear me? Over.'

'I'm still here,' Willow replied. 'The comms gear from Alard's place has been destroyed. Alec wants you in Tropolis does he? You've got to get to that video message.'

Luca sighed. 'We haven't made it into Tropolis yet, but I know that if we do get in, we are the best hope that Campion and Outside will be free.'

'And that the Tropolites will stop suffering.' Willow's voice could not disguise her mistrust.

'I'm not going through this again,' Luca said. 'If we get into Tropolis, either through Alec or some other way,' Luca glanced at his father, 'Campion and Outside has a good chance that they will be free.'

There was another pause. 'Then you should go.'

Luca laughed a little. 'If only we could.'

'What's stopping you? Are you alright?' Willow asked evidently worried.

Luca shrugged. 'We are with Campion and the Outsiders. We are in their camp.'

Willow was quiet for a moment. 'Is it safe to talk?' she whispered.

'It is now!' Luca laughed. 'I'm glad you took your time in telling us you had made the village safe though.'

'Why?'

Luca huffed. 'We've just been told that we won't be going into the city. That they are sending in someone more qualified for the job.'

'You'll be safe.'

'That's not the point ...'

Amil said loudly, 'That's exactly the point.'

'Who is that with you?' Willow asked.

Luca waited and looked up at Amil. His father put out his hand. 'You have to squeeze the button to talk to her,' Luca instructed.

Amil's hand trembled as he took the tapper and squeezed it. 'It's your Amil.'

There was no reply.

'Try again, dad.'

'Willow?' he said gently. 'I'm so glad that you are alive. I've missed you terribly. I'm so proud of your bravery in Campion today. Isn't Luca just what we'd always wished? He has so much courage and strength. He is incredible.' Amil paused.

'Amil?' Willow's voice cracked with emotion. 'I'm so sorry, my love.'

Amil's tears ran freely. 'I'm sorry I sent you, its my fault. I'm to blame for what happened to you. I'm sorry I never came for you. I'm sorry I never took Luca away from Outside. I've been lost without you.'

Luca bowed his head. He felt like he was intruding. He began to shift uneasily and was about to leave when Amil sat next to him and put his arm around him.

'Stop that! It's not your fault,' Willow said with certainty and then added a little sadly, 'I should have found a way ...'

'We can talk about that later,' Amil said laughing a little.

'There'll only be a later if Eban can get that message played,' Willow replied. Eban nodded when Amil looked at him. 'Who is stopping them from going in? If others can get in, surely they can too.'

'Griffin's plan is a good one,' Amil said.

'Griffin?' Willow asked. 'Who put him in charge?'

Eban began to laugh. 'Griffin is good at this stuff.'

'Since when?' Willow replied. 'It doesn't matter. Luca, Eban and Mercy need to get in. Oh, and Kelsee too. How about the route you took out of Tropolis? You could show them the way in.'

Luca raised his eyebrows at his father and began to chuckle.

'Willow, he's our son. We need to keep him safe.'

'Yes, and we've done such a good job of that already!' she replied sarcastically. 'You can get them in safely, I know that. And Alec is there too. Did you know Alec is alive? He helped Luca before. He won't be alone.'

'But what if I can't get them in safely?'

'What if you do?' Willow answered quickly. 'We saw more drones flying over. I don't think the powers of Tropolis will leave us alone until we are out of the way.'

'I didn't think I'd get him back.'

'But you did. We did,' Willow breathed heavily into the tapper. 'You know better than anyone how the Prize trains the kids. You know that it breaks them before it rebuilds them. But it didn't do that to Luca. It didn't do that to Luca, Mercy or Eban. I think they are strong enough for this. I think they have to be strong enough for this because they are our best chance at being a family again.'

Amil looked up into the branches of the evergreen, deliberately avoiding Luca's confused gaze. Luca watched as his father processed what his mother had put before them. How, he wondered, could his father know about the Prize better than anyone?

'Amil? Are you still there?' she asked quietly. 'I love him, and I know he can do this.'

'I'm going to make the right choice because I love him too,' Amil replied. 'I'll take them in.'

Chapter 14

Amil took the four of them to the very edge of the woods and out to the coastal path that ran along the base of the cliff. They moved without question or being noticed. Luca supposed that Griffin had called all those that might have seen them as out of the ordinary into his own planning meeting.

The bay was beautiful and calm, but the concrete path showed the potential and violent power of the ocean. Pebbles had been tossed far over the flint wall that edged the beach and onto the narrow road where the last houses stood.

Luca peered over the divide. The beach was riveted with rows of smooth rocks covered in limp and stranded seaweed. Further ahead there were stairs that led down to the beach; the treads had been broken and curved over time.

Amil pointed to a walled section much further along the path. 'There's the marina.' He looked behind him. 'I'd prefer to do this at night, but I think Griffin would have his own team by then.' Amil grabbed Luca's elbow. 'If I can get you to the rubbish loading bays, can you find your way from there? Do you remember the route?'

'Where will you be?' Mercy asked.

'I'll slow you down,' Amil replied, 'And besides, if Griffin wants more people sent in, well, I might be able to hold them back for a while, until you have made it safe for us all.'

Luca ran his hand through his hair. It seemed a huge pressure when his father put it that way. He looked towards the marina and to the wall that was so different to that of Outside.

Luca recalled how he had learned who Kelsee really was just the other side of the marina wall as they were escaping from the Prize. She had proved that her name did not make her a certain person and it did not dictate who she really was. She had discovered a different design. The revelation had been shocking to him in that she claimed to be part of Harland's family at all. Luca was glad that he had brought her with them. He thought about the things that they had done. They may not have motivated and gathered the people of Campion and Outside together like Mercy and Eban, but they had found the truth about Harland and Hutchings and they had found the Emundabit cube. Perhaps it was right that they would be part of this. Perhaps the part they had to play was important after all.

He glanced at her now. She had zipped up her jacket as high as it would go. She hadn't spoken for so long that Luca was worried for her. As he studied her he saw pain in her eyes. She kept rubbing her ear against her shoulder but didn't take her focus from their destination. Luca did not know what to do. Had grief swept her away? He tried to smile reassuringly at her, but she was focussed elsewhere.

He stared at the marina wall. It did not completely encompass its inhabitants but protected them from the possible storms and raging waves. Its narrow gap enabled the boats and rubbish barge to come and go as they pleased. Luca understood why the Campion leadership and crew had initially chosen the vast river mouth that would have taken them to the heart of the city over the marina. Entering one by one by the narrow gateway would have been a risk after being pushed back so heavily before. The small bay was ideal. They could enter in strength and overpower whoever was here, had there been anyone left to protect it.

It was strange that this on-the-edge community had already left their homes before Campion arrived. Luca wondered how they knew to leave before the decision to even land had been made.

'What happened when you came into the bay?' Luca asked. 'Griffin gave the impression that there were no people there.'

'No one!' Amil replied. 'They left in a hurry though, as you saw. Many of the houses were unlocked, and lights on.'

Eban butted in and pulled Amil to a stop. 'Any computers, tablets or comms gear in them?'

Amil shook his head. 'There were screens linked to the Network, but nothing else.'

Eban let go and shrugged. 'It was worth a shot.'

'I guess,' Luca said, 'They saw the broadcast and decided to get into the city knowing that they were vulnerable out on the edge of things.'

'That gives me an idea to get you in unnoticed,' Amil said as they approached a tiny cottage that faced out to sea at the very outskirts of the community. 'I heard someone from Campion suggesting to Major Thomas that we go into Tropolis dressed as Tropolites. The plan was, of course, flawed because there are so many of us. But in your case, it could work.'

Amil pushed open the door and began to climb the stairs. 'There'll be clothes here. White clothes.'

Luca entered the bright bedroom. The room was simpler than the contestants' rooms in the city but still had a distinct Tropolis flavour. The cupboards and drawers in the bedroom of this tidy home were filled with freshly laundered and pressed white outfits. The inhabitants had been fairly slim and so the clothes would be ideal.

Luca began to feel nauseous as he tried to find something that fitted. It reminded him of his first experience in Tropolis where his identity as an Outsider was stripped away. Luca ran his hand through his hair. It was still short, and he had grown used to it, but it was styled in Tropolite neatness that had been created for his Prize persona.

The trousers were a little too long and baggy but by turning up the legs and wearing a belt, they were manageable. Luca knew that he couldn't lose any of the items that he had gleaned on his journey so far. He clipped the radio to the belt and popped the Emundabit cube, tapper and torch into his pockets.

The yellowed piece of paper was in Luca's jacket. He knew that they would have to leave anything that was not regarded as Tropolite behind so he pulled the paper out and began to unfold it.

Mercy knocked on the door. 'Are you nearly done?' she asked.

Eban looked up from fastening his shoes and caught Luca with the paper. 'Nearly!' he replied and then whispered, 'What's that?'

Luca shoved it into his pocket, shook his head and opened the door. Mercy hadn't picked out a flowing dress like she had worn in Tropolis – instead she wore joggers, but her hair was combed and tied back in a distinctly Tropolite style. Kelsee stood behind her, looking the most natural in white out of all of them. Did he really think her as anything other than a Tropolite? He pulled at the sleeve on his shirt and sighed. The closer they got to Tropolis the further away she seemed from him. He began to grasp at reasons for her distance. He started to feel ill at the thought that perhaps coming back to Tropolis was changing her. He took a steadying breath and really studied her. Her slightly wild hair had been tamed and plaited, the cut to her cheek had been re-dressed but she still didn't stand tall. This wasn't her becoming stronger at all. Luca tried to focus on what he knew to be true of her.

Luca watched her closely, she was different, the familiar clothing hadn't brought back the Kelsee he had known, she seemed to still be hiding somewhere. Perhaps the shadow of grief had taken her under its wing. Luca wanted to push it back and find her again but had no idea how to do that. He had lived in that place for so long that he had made it a comfortable home, and even his mother proving to be alive hadn't really helped him. Distraction and keeping busy had been the things that kept the symptoms distant.

Amil called to them from the foot of the stairs. When they appeared, he nodded in appreciation of the borrowed plan. 'It might just work,' he said. Amil was also dressed in white and it unsettled Luca to see his father in the colour that he officially belonged. 'Hopefully we can get away with the shoes, but you'll have to do away with those Campion jackets. Grab another jumper if you can't find any coats. There are none down here.'

Kelsee was visibly upset when she joined the others at the door. Luca knew that she would have been searching for that folded paper that had been safely tucked away in her jacket but was now in his pocket. She had pretended that it hadn't existed before so wouldn't own up to it now, but he didn't want to tell her that he had it because he wanted her to trust him. Of course, now that he had the item, it would prove to her that he wasn't trustworthy at all. He wished that he had just let her tell him in her time what it was all about. It almost burned in his pocket. He didn't look at her and tried to hurry them along. Kelsee grabbed a scarf from the peg and wrapped it around her neck and face.

A few moments later and they were out by the sea. The path that had skirted the bay now hugged the growing cliffs. It would have been wide enough for Alard's jeep, but Luca didn't think that it was designed for vehicles. Perhaps the people of Tropolis used to just walk along beside the sea, enjoying the view, without any worries or cares. His stomach tightened as he considered the possibility of just walking for pleasure, of not needing to do anything to survive. It was so foreign. But then he wondered if the Tropolites of recent years had even done that. The fatigue had been spreading and he had witnessed the lack of people out on the streets of Tropolis. It seemed that even his own bitterness and jealousy for a perfect and secure life was tainted or was not real. He sighed. Outside had its wall but so did Tropolis.

Further along, the path widened a little and several wooden huts stood in neat and orderly lines facing out to sea. They were pristine white, but their doors had been carefully painted in several different hues. They were curious buildings to find in the middle of nowhere. In between these huts, a wide staircase rose towards the cliff face before it separated into two, each flight of stairs snaking its way to the top of the cliff.

'This way,' Amil said and he pulled himself up the stairs using the iron rail. 'If we keep to the coastal path any longer, the security guards at the marina are likely to see us.'

Kelsee tugged at Luca's arm. 'I can't go any further. I need to go back.'

Luca turned to face her fully as the others followed Amil. 'What do you mean? I can't leave you with Major Thomas. I want you to be with me.'

'I just can't.' Kelsee said lowering her gaze.

Luca bowed his head. 'It isn't lost,' he admitted. 'I've got it.' He pulled out the yellowed paper and gave it to Kelsee. She looked confused. 'I took it.'

'Why?'

'You were hiding it.'

She held it tightly and then put it into her pocket.

'What is it?' Luca asked.

'It doesn't matter.'

Luca tilted his head to one side. 'I think it does. You were ready to go back to get it.'

Kelsee shrugged and looked down at her hands. She fidgeted with a thread from her jumper. 'A birth certificate.' Kelsee looked up at Luca. 'But that isn't why I wanted to go back.'

Luca was grateful that Kelsee hadn't pushed him aside and was keen to change the subject. 'I know that you are finding this tough, but you need to be with people who care about you.'

Kelsee closed her eyes and a tear fell to the ground. 'I'm frightened,' she admitted.

Luca pulled her into a hug and kissed her head. 'You have no idea how much I want to tell you it is all going to be alright, but I can't.'

'I can't stop thinking about it all going wrong,' Kelsee whispered. 'I can't be in Tropolis. The closer I get the more I think about all the bad stuff.'

'We're here,' Luca said kindly. 'Mercy and Eban are amazing at that stuff.'

'I'm frightened for you,' Kelsee said hiding her face in Luca's shoulder.

'Then come with us,' he said. 'Come and be my protection.'

'I don't think I can be.' Kelsee pushed herself away from Luca. 'You don't understand. I'm frightened that I'll hurt you.'

Luca reached for her. 'You wouldn't hurt me. I trust you.'

'Then you shouldn't trust me. You should go into Tropolis without me. You need to get that video shown and stop this.' Kelsee held her ears and turned away.

Luca glanced at the others who were almost a quarter of the way up the staircase and then turned back to Kelsee. He put his hand on her shoulder. 'I do trust you. Why would you say that I shouldn't? What's going on?'

She turned, her lips and chin were trembling. 'I'm ...' She lowered her voice to a whisper. 'I'm not good, Luca. I keep thinking these terrible thoughts, its like I'm hearing them scream at me, I keep wanting to hurt you and to stop the others.' She put her hands out to create some distance between them. 'I don't know why, but I can't block the thoughts from coming.'

'Thoughts to hurt me?'

'I can be fine, then suddenly it feels like this other voice takes over and makes me want to do horrible stuff.' Kelsee refused to look at Luca. 'I can't be trusted. You'd be safer without me.'

'Have I done anything?'

'It's not you, you've been so kind to me, you've been the only person who has ever really wanted to know me. I don't know where these thoughts come from, but they are loud and getting clearer.'

'The closer we get to Tropolis?' Luca asked.

Kelsee nodded. 'I can't go there. I need to get as far away from there as possible.'

'And I would come with you,' Luca began.

'But you have to go in and stop Hutchings.'

'Yes, I do,' Luca said, 'But that is not what I was thinking. These thoughts are getting louder and clearer you say?' Kelsee bit her lip and nodded. 'Do these thoughts have anything to do with what you are doing or talking about or were thinking up until that moment?'

'No!' Kelsee cried out. 'I don't want to hurt you!' Kelsee pulled her hands to her chest. 'Not in here, not where it matters. That's why I've got to let you go.'

'Then you need to listen to that, because that is who you are.' Luca approached her and she stepped away. 'Those other thoughts, they aren't you, are they?'

'Not at all, but they are in me somewhere.'

'I think they are in you but not who you are. I remember that you said that Tropolis wanted to chip the population, but that it didn't happen.'

'No, it didn't happen.'

'But you have had injections, right? I mean you have been given the cure several times.'

'Of course. I've also had the vaccine.'

'Vaccine?'

'They thought they had created the vaccine against the fatigue and everyone got a shot. Of course it didn't work.'

'The whole of Tropolis got a vaccine? When was this?'

'All of us. I was probably about ten or eleven.' Kelsee covered her mouth. 'It wasn't a vaccine was it?'

Luca shook his head. 'I don't think so.' Luca grabbed Kelsee's hand and pulled her towards the stairs. They ran up to the others.

'Eban! Mercy!' Luca called. They stopped and waited on a landing. 'The Tropolites have been chipped.'

Mercy frowned. 'What makes you say that?'

'Kelsee has been ...' Luca began. He looked at Kelsee and wasn't sure what to say.

'I've been having these thoughts that aren't my thoughts,' Kelsee said, a lightness coming over her that Luca hadn't seen for a while. 'All of Tropolis were given a vaccine quite a few years ago, they told us it was for the fatigue. Everyone had it, but people still got sick.'

Luca nodded and licked his lips. 'You know how the tablets worked, with the sound going straight into our heads when we were watching those instruction videos?' Mercy and Eban nodded.

Eban pointed at Kelsee. 'It's not thoughts is it? You've been actually hearing things, haven't you? That's why that dream was so bad and oh,' Eban said scratching his head, 'when those Tropolite drones flew over you heard more.' Eban frowned. 'Tropolis is broadcasting thoughts! That is... urgh! That is enough!'

Mercy pointed back to the bay. 'Do you think that is why that place was empty? Is Tropolis invading everyone's thoughts?'

'Not everyone,' Luca said. 'We're not having them, are we?'

'We are Outsiders,' Amil said. 'At least you are. I left a long time before that, but Outsiders have their own chips.'

'Campion disabled ours.' Luca stared wide eyed. 'What about Josetta and the army? Did theirs get disabled by Campion?'

Mercy patted Luca's arm. 'They have Outsider chips from when they lived in Outside. I think that Tropolis wouldn't waste that kind of technology on a group of people that it thought was contained and under control.'

'We have no idea what happens at the end of the Prize. Perhaps they get a new chip then.' Luca turned to Eban. 'Look at Thickset, or Seth, he's under Tropolis control.'

Eban shrugged. 'He was always drawn that way, Luca. He didn't need a chip to adjust his thoughts.' He sighed. 'Certain people are clearly drawn there naturally, look at Atticus.'

Amil leaned in. 'I don't think that Josetta has that chip,' he said. 'She wouldn't need it.' Amil began to climb the stairs again.

'Why not?' asked Luca. 'Surely, if the rest of Tropolis was chipped, why not Prize winners?'

Amil stopped and but did not turn to face his son. He paused before he answered. 'Tropolis were vaccinating their people. Those from Outside didn't come down with the fatigue so didn't need a vaccine.' Amil took another step. 'But as soon as I take you in, I can go back and do something about it.'

Kelsee spoke up. 'This doesn't stop what I am thinking though.'

'No,' Luca said and rubbed her hand with his thumb. 'But it does reveal what Tropolis is thinking and that might be of use to us.'

'But I could hurt you.' Kelsee was still upset.

Luca sighed. 'Yes, but I don't think that you will let yourself do that. Like I said before, I trust you.' He pulled her to the next flight of stairs and they began to climb together.

Amil was panting when he got to the top of the stairs. Luca was concerned. 'Can you go any further?' he asked. His father batted away the question and moved on.

At the top of the cliff there was an arc of benches facing out to sea and a wider tarmacked road beyond them. The wind howled, and Luca wrapped his arms around himself.

'We've got to get out of this,' he shouted.

Amil gestured to walk alongside the road. It seemed that they had arrived at the pinnacle of the cliff face as the road swept down towards more houses some distance away.

'We'll be seen!' Luca called out.

'Only if these people weren't summoned to Tropolis,' Amil replied. 'And I have a feeling that they were. What will they see if they are here?'

Luca looked at himself. They would see Tropolites. They were hiding in full sight.

The temperature was dropping and the chill from the wind was not altered by the late sunlight.

Amil had a plan to get them to the rubbish chute into Tropolis, but Luca wasn't expecting to be walking into a narrow road away from the sea and the marina. Amil's confidence at the lack of Tropolites this far away from the main city centre was rewarded, although it was disturbing at the same time.

When Amil took them further away from their goal Luca protested.

'We need to circle round,' Amil reassured him. 'We need to come into the marina as if we have come from the city.'

Luca brushed down his clothing, hoping that they would blend in.

Amil wove in and out of streets, pushing his way deeper into the Tropolis suburb.

The buildings here were much denser and tightly packed. They lacked the clean style of the city skyscrapers, but they were typically Tropolite in style. The white render and sharp lines were not interrupted by plants or character like that of Campion's ground level three. They were also taller, often four or five storeys high.

Luca was distracted by the unnerving stillness of the community. The street was not heavily populated. There were some Tropolites that shuffled quickly along the streets and disappeared around corners while others looked out of the windows, or at least glanced at the friends. Luca assumed that his small band of friends were not seen as a threat in their advance, appearance or numbers, so they were dismissed. No one seemed to give the intruders a second look. Their Tropolis disguise was enough for now. These Tropolites were not going to harm them.

To be in a place where people lived was unsettling for Luca. He had been so used to the hovels of Outside and their lack of belonging together. Then he had seen the people gathering as part of Campion but the warmth that their community claimed to have had not shown outwardly and was awkward even in the bay. Luca frowned as he considered why he felt so disturbed, perhaps Tropolis was more similar to Outside and Campion than he wanted to consider.

He had even experienced the home of the richest of Tropolis at Harland's mansion with its ancient heirlooms, colour and warmth but no family. He wasn't sure what he was expecting of the real Tropolis after being exposed to the Prize environment, but he had never really considered the way these people lived. He had previously thought of the richness and privilege, and he had desired it when he entered the Prize, but now he saw it and how the people reacted to threat and wondered which group had the toughest deal. Tropolites were fearful and under the control of their wealth. They feared it being taken and had been ready to defend it. He wondered if it had been Outside, would the people have been any different. Luca bit his lip and sighed. Outsiders were people of poverty and had spent their lives grabbing at what they could get their hands on because no one would ever give it to them. But perhaps the Tropolites were not that different to them after all. They would not let go of what they had, fearful that it would be taken forever.

Kelsee put her hands to her ears.

'What is it?' Mercy asked.

Kelsee's eyes filled with tears. 'I think they want us here.'

'What do you mean?' Eban asked.

'I don't know how to explain,' Kelsee began, 'But I think they want me to bring you into the city, it's as if I really want to go there.' Kelsee looked wide eyed at Luca. 'We shouldn't be doing this. This is what Hutchings wants.'

Amil patted her arm. 'We're not going to the centre,' he said.

Luca put his arm around Kelsee's shoulder. He looked around feeling like he was being watched. 'We've got to get out of here,' Luca whispered. 'Dad, we need to get to the marina.'

Amil nodded and took a sharp right at the next road and they found themselves walking down a slight hill. The tall buildings either side afforded a narrow view of the sea. They hurried towards the end of the road and the horizon opened wider until they were back on the coastal beach road.

Luca scanned for the marina and they had passed it in their weaving through the streets. Amil had brought them back to the sea – only this time they would be entering the marina from the Tropolis side.

The lack of any others on the road this close to the marina made the group conspicuous but there was little choice.

Amil took them down a short flight of stairs, away from the residential houses and a lower path almost right on the beach. Luca felt more confident. They were protected from being seen by the occupants of houses from this route and the marina faced away from them, so it felt as if the security would also be focused on the bay further away.

They approached the marina wall that jutted out to sea but was easily one third of the height of Outside. The dinging and tinkling of the ropes on the masts floated on the air with the calls of seagulls. The calm sound going against the drumming of Luca's heart.

The path forked. One wider road led around the side of the marina and was barred, and the other route went through a brick lined archway that was cut into the wall. The short tunnel had a slight decline and was lit with spots of light. The walls were crisp white except for the steel hand rails. A gust of cold wind blew dust and the stench of rubbish into Luca's face.

Kelsee held the scarf over her nose.

Amil peered out from the tunnel and then beckoned them to follow. There were no signs of any security and Luca could feel the sense of hope rising. The path swept around a large open paved area marked with multiple rectangular bays. Some of these had chains and posts with names and reserved parking signs. The friends kept as close as they could to the ramped road that curved above them. The road must have broken from the higher coastal highway before feeding into the marina and terminating at the parking zones.

A large stainless-steel, open arch gated the paved walkway that fronted the brightly lit shops. Luca remembered the extravagance and richness of the window displays from when Kelsee had brought them to her grandfather's boat after they had escaped from the Prize, but he refused to be distracted by them this time. They had arrived at the opposite end of the parade of shopfronts. Kelsee ran forward, keeping herself close to the windows and darted into the alley that ran between some of the buildings.

'She knows where she is going?' Amil asked.

Luca nodded. 'She never was like other Tropolites. She has been watching what has happened to Outside and just didn't know what she could do to help.'

Kelsee peered around the alley end and ushered them to join her.

'I can't go much further,' Amil said. 'It will take too long for me to travel down that tunnel to the contestants' building and back. I need to return to the bay and hold Griffin off. I need to give you a chance.'

Mercy hugged him. 'You're leaving us?'

'Just think of it as rallying the troops so they are ready to follow you.'

Eban hugged Amil too. 'Thank you, Amil,' he said. 'You are a courageous man to come back here.'

Amil nodded but his eyes looked sad.

Eban and Mercy ran to join Kelsee.

'Please stay safe, Luca.'

Luca snorted. 'I'll try.'

Amil turned away.

'Dad,' Luca said quickly knowing that this might be his last opportunity to ask. Amil turned back. 'Something Willow said,' Luca began.

'Please don't ask me, son.'

'I need to know.' Luca opened his hands towards his father. 'Why would you know about the Prize better than anyone else?'

Amil shook his head and lowered his gaze. 'Please, Luca!'

'What is it?' Luca asked. 'You are my father and I barely know you.'

'You won't want to know me. I want you to think better of me.'

Luca considered for a moment. Was there anything that Amil had done that had been worse than what Luca had already endured? To leave him to look after the both of them when his mother had *died*, to remain silent about who he really was? Luca had to know the truth.

Luca asked again. 'I won't be able to concentrate on what I need to do if I am left wondering about it.' The sound of his argument was out of tune and Luca knew that he was being manipulative. 'I'll think all the worst things.'

'And they won't be bad enough,' Amil replied sadly.

'You can't know that!'

Amil took a deep breath. 'Please come back to me, Luca, or at least, after you hear about me, come back for your mother. I do love you.' Luca waited for Amil to finish. 'I was on the planning committee for the Prize. I invented the hallucinogenic and fixing drug for the Connections Test. I've trapped more Outsiders than you and I will ever know.'

Luca stood back and looked at his father. There was a numbness and fog in his thinking.

'I'm sorry,' Amil said quietly. 'I saw what it did that first year, how successful it was in the eyes of the committee and how they used it beyond what I had designed it for.' Amil stepped towards Luca. 'It's why the contestants never needed to be chipped by Tropolis; they had been redesigned by the drug already.' Amil lowered his head. 'Can you forgive me?'

Harland's voice echoed through Luca's memory. Forgive him? Had Amil been the one that had trapped him on that church floor in unreasonable fear? Luca focused on his father and took a deep breath and shook his head.

'If you need me to say it, then I forgive you,' Luca began. 'But I don't need to do it. If they used it in a way that you didn't design it, that is not your fault.'

'Really?' Amil asked looking up at his son. 'But I made it, I created it.'

'In your hands it would have been something else.'

'I hope you are right,' Amil said.

Luca reached out and touched his father's hands. 'You came to Outside to punish yourself.'

'And instead I found Willow.' Amil smiled. 'Hardly what I deserved.'

'I wish you had told me earlier, it would have been so much easier if you had.' Luca thought for a moment and wondered if he had been told the truth, would he have understood before he had been through what he had. He was a changed person now.

Amil shook his head. 'I wish I had seen you for who you are.' He grasped Luca's hand. 'You are remarkable.' He pulled him close and hugged him tightly. 'I love you, son,' he whispered.

Luca turned to see the others waiting. 'I've got to go.' He smiled at his father and his heart burned brightly for him. 'I'll try to stay safe.' Luca began to move away but then added. 'If you were able to create it, you might be able to undo it,' Luca hesitated, 'Or at least counteract it. I love you too, dad.'

He ran over to the alley and turned to see his father. Amil leaned against the wall but Luca could see it wasn't due to weakness that he needed support. Amil rubbed his hand down the side of his face and smiled gently at his son. He waved and nodded.

'I could do that!' Amil called out.

Luca smiled widely and waved before he turned to hide in the darkness that the passage offered.

His father had been part of the Prize and had suffered enough without him piling more onto him. It was a strange sensation and Luca felt that odd lightness and the rush of emotion.

'Is everything alright?' Mercy asked.

Luca smiled.

The path was gritty under foot and the sound was small in comparison to the raised voices ahead. The friends approached the other end of the alley with caution. Luca recalled that behind all the prosperity of Tropolis, its yachts and expensive shops, there were the services. The marina docked the wealth and the rubbish barges, but the waste was kept from view. At the end of this backstreet, Luca and Eban had escaped from being boiled in the cleaning shed where the carriages that carried the rubbish were cleaned having deposited their load in the waiting barge.

Wafts from concentrated decaying rubbish pummelled Luca's senses. The violent intensity was out of place and sickening. The wooden gates of the cleaning shed had been firmly shut on their last visit were now open wide. Waste flowed out of them and covered the entire walkway in a sinking heap. If the carriages had got to the cleaning shed, they should have been empty, but they were still full. There were many Maglev refuse containers queued up further along the rail with nowhere to go. There was a barge waiting at the dockside rail overflowing with its pungent load. A second carriage had been caught above it in a tipping position and was trapped from moving by the amount of waste that was already piled up. There were several white clad security guards with their dark belts and hats surrounding the mess. Their clothes were stained, and their voices raised in frustration.

Luca withdrew and slumped against the wall. With the route into the city overflowing with rubbish and obviously blocked with waste they would struggle to get in, and that wasn't taking into account the concentration of security at the single-entry point. There was no way in.

Chapter 15

One by one the others joined him in the shadow of the alley.

'Any ideas?' Luca asked brushing the dirt from his hands.

'Is that the only way in?' Mercy asked.

Luca snorted. 'It's the only way we know.' He peered down the backstreet. 'We could catch up with my father.'

'I think this was the only route he knew too,' Eban replied. 'I don't think he even came under the city like we did.'

'I don't really remember how I got to the boat from the death room,' Mercy recalled.

Kelsee rubbed her neck. 'We can try going through the city. I can take us. I know the way. My grandfather would bring me out to the boats every weekend when I was little.'

Eban ruffled his hair. 'It's a good plan.'

Luca sighed. 'It's our only plan apart from going back.' Luca raised his eyebrows, 'And I don't want to do that. Griffin is going to cut us out even though we are the best hope.'

Mercy began to walk down the alley towards the shops and boats. 'We don't have to do everything, but since we are here, it would be a waste not to at least try.' She turned and smiled widely. Luca couldn't help but return it.

Since all the security was busy with the refuse incident, the friends had no difficulty in leaving the marina the way they came. Kelsee was certain that the beach side path ran parallel with the main road and they kept to it for as long as she was confident.

'The thoughts are stronger here,' Kelsee said as she walked ahead with Luca. 'They are more intense.'

Luca squeezed her hand.

'I'm much better though,' Kelsee said reassuringly. 'It's as if my knowing that they are there and why they are there has made them so stupid and outlandish.' Kelsee leaned into Luca. 'They may be stronger, but that just makes them even more out of place somehow.' She laughed, and Luca was content with the sound. 'They don't make any sense at all because I know that they aren't me.'

'I'm glad you told me,' Luca said.

'I'm glad you listened,' Kelsee replied. 'I am still a bit baffled by them, but I'm trying to check them out against the truth.' Kelsee sighed and shrugged. 'I wonder how long it has been going on.'

Kelsee took them up onto the main road and to a large statue that stood tall above them. The person it represented was simple and elegant but not anyone that Luca could recognise. The white marble had been marked by the passing birds and the artwork punctuated the end of a wide, tree lined road that terminated at the beach front but stretched out long and straight ahead of them.

'This way,' Kelsee said.

Every building on this stretch of road was grand and unique. There were some that were set back from the neatly paved highway with long and immaculate green lawns. Others had chosen to dazzle their neighbour with lights set into the paths or walls. One building had a roof supported by stone pillars. Luca viewed them as lavish and extreme. They had character and individuality, but each house was white.

The trees on the parade were bare, since, no doubt, the leaves had been torn from them by the strong wind blowing up from the sea. There was no leaf litter or mess though, everything was tidy and contained. It was unnaturally clean. Luca cautiously peered into windows but there was no one to be seen. The road was deserted.

When they had reached the other end of the road, a huge stone building, with dozens of sparkling windows, spanned the entire width. It was decorated with carved cornices and ornate plaques. Three massive arches that pierced the barrier allowed for vehicles to pass through to the other side. Luca and the others held back. Where they stood they were alone, but just through the stonework there were lots of Tropolites filing past all travelling in the same direction.

Luca approached nervously. He stayed close to the stone and could feel his hands shaking. Kelsee pulled him to a quicker pace. She smiled, her chin held high. As she stepped out to the other side she winced and scrunched her eyes shut.

'What is it?' Luca asked. His voice was loud, and he realised that despite the busyness of the street, no one else was talking. The only sound was the tapping of urgent feet. He turned to see Mercy's brow furrowed and confusion in her eyes.

Luca leaned closer to Kelsee and whispered. 'Can I help?'

Kelsee groaned a little as she shook her head. 'It's so loud here,' she almost shouted.

Eban rushed forward. 'Kelsee, you need to keep your voice down,' he whispered. 'They'll notice ...' But even as he said it, Luca knew that Eban was wrong. No one was paying any attention to them.

Luca watched as one Tropolite woman with a red belt and bright red lipstick stopped suddenly. He thought that she had seen them, but she just turned back and began walking the other way. After a few paces she blinked a few times, then turned again and resumed walking in the original direction.

'What is going on?' Luca asked Mercy and Eban.

Eban had stepped out into the crowd but they just diverted around him without a complaint or any collision. 'This is not normal,' he said.

The Tropolites stared blankly, many of them showing distinct signs of the fatigue. Although they walked with purpose, many appeared weary and lacking in strength. Others had dark circles under their eyes and pallid complexions.

The skyscrapers of the city centre were close by. The tops of the nearest buildings almost grazed the walls of the steel and glass structures. Luca knew that they needed to go towards them but the majority of the Tropolites seemed to be heading in the opposite direction and that did not sit comfortably with him.

'I don't like this one bit,' said Mercy. 'Why are all these people here?'

None of them had an answer.

A glass and steel roof spanned an open space. It may have been a couple of storeys high, but in comparison to everything else, it was squat. Several Maglev tracks were neatly lined up next to platforms and at each there was an inactive Maglev. The station was completely empty of people, but a voice echoed through the space.

A large screen was mounted on the station wall. Luca pulled Kelsee away from the Tropolite herds and into the space. She resisted for a moment.

A young and completely alive Harland Barret was on the Network screen.

'... stay in your homes and defend yourself. We are doing all we can to protect you and our precious Tropolis.'

'That is horrendous!' Luca tutted.

'Thank you all for your co-operation. Please stay tuned to the Network and we will inform you of any further updates.'

There was then a silky lady's voice that spoke out over the Network symbol that span lazily on screen. 'That was a news update from Tropolis Head of House. We will now resume programming. Thank you for your patience.' A moment later and a quirky theme tune filled the station alongside a flash of images.

Luca moved away. 'If they are telling people to stay in their homes, why are so many on the streets?'

'Perhaps they are going home,' Mercy suggested.

'That wasn't my grandfather,' Kelsee said sadly. She took a deep breath and composed herself. 'And the Network didn't say go home. It said to circle the city.' She paused. 'Listen, there it goes again.'

Luca took Kelsee's face in his hands. 'Is that what you hear?'

'Yes,' she agreed. 'Circle the city. There it goes again.'

Luca looked at her in the eyes. 'Listen again, Kelsee. Try not to hear the Network. What do you really hear?'

Kelsee winced and grunted. 'I don't hear anything but that stupid show. But it was there. Was it the chip? Do you think everyone is hearing *circle the city?*'

Mercy looked at the people marching by. 'I think everyone hears that.'

'What about defending themselves, Kelsee?' Eban asked. 'Are the chips transmitting that?'

'Not at all,' Kelsee said.

Luca peered back at the screen. There were several people chatting and laughing with presenter Nolan Smythe. It made no sense. Why would the Network broadcast one thing yet the chips tell the Tropolites to do something else and not reinforce it?

'We need to get to that media suite,' Luca said pointing his finger at the tall steel buildings.

Knowing that the Tropolites were somehow focused on their task made their journey into the city easy. They did not fear being caught or attacked since there was no instruction to do so. Kelsee listened in briefly; the command remained the same.

The buildings around the central area of the city were so much taller. The crowds seemed to spiral into the centre but there was still an eerie silence to their marching. It reminded Luca of the Prize and the disturbing test that he had endured.

Suddenly there was a scream from behind them. A middle-aged woman came running towards them across the small courtyard, her hair wild and her Tropolite clothes untidy.

Eban stood in front of the group.

'What's happening?' she shouted. 'Why is all this happening?'

'What's happening with you?' Eban asked.

'I was staying inside, just like the Network said. I saw you, you aren't like everyone else. What is going on?'

'We're trying to work that out too,' Kelsee said quietly.

'Kelsee Barret!' the woman screamed again, only this time there was no horror in it. 'The real Kelsee Barret!'

Kelsee nodded. 'That's right!'

'Oh, just wait until I tell ...' She paused and looked around her, her eyes wide again with fear. 'I want to tell them, but no one will listen!'

'I know,' Kelsee said. 'Go back into your home and stay safe.' Kelsee gave the lady a hug. 'Please go back inside, we'll get this all worked out.'

'But the Outsiders are coming to kill us. This is their fault.'

Luca balled his fists. Kelsee smiled sweetly at the woman. 'The Outsiders are going to save us. You see this.' She gestured to the blank faced crowds, 'Tropolis is causing this. We need the Outsiders and they are coming to help us.'

'I don't want those filthy scavengers helping me!' the woman said.

'Then you will have to live like this!' Eban replied.

'And who are you?' she mocked.

'I'm an Outsider and Prize contestant.'

'No!' she said looking more closely. 'You're the one that threatened us on the Network.' The woman growled and curved her back. Her hands came up as if she were a wild animal with claws. 'I should kill you now!' she hissed.

She jumped at Eban and grabbed him tightly by the throat. The movement was so quick that none of them were ready to defend him. Eban tried to pull her hands away but she squeezed tighter.

Chapter 16

Luca dashed forward and pulled at the woman's arms. He unbalanced her, but her grip was so strong that Eban stumbled to the ground.

'Let go!' Mercy demanded as she attemped to prise the woman's fingers away.

Eban's eyes were wide and he struggled for breath. He knelt before his assailant and struggled to free himself.

The woman stood over Eban, more energised and determined.

Kelsee grabbed the woman's waist and tried to pull her away but she would not be moved. 'Leave him alone!'she shouted and then grasped a handful of the attacker's hair and yanked hard.

A loud bang rang across the courtyard and the woman fell limply to the ground. Luca stepped back and crouched low. Kelsee screamed and hid behind him.

Luca scanned the square and Josetta stepped into view.

'Are you all okay?' she called, and she jogged towards them followed by four of her fellow army recruits.

'What are you doing here?' Eban rasped. He coughed and rubbed his throat. 'Did you just save me?'

'I think so, Eban.' Josetta's voice quavered. 'Is Griffin's team already here?' Luca asked looking behind her.

Josetta shook her head. 'We weren't sure about Griffin's plan and a number from the crew thought it best to keep track of you when you disappeared.' She offered her hands to Luca and Kelsee and they stood up. 'We thought if you were going to work from the centre of it all, we might be able to help by starting with our families and friends. We have people we love here and wanted them to know that we hadn't turned against them.'

'Have you found them?'

Josetta looked at the people filing by in the nearby street. 'I'm not sure we will.' Josetta scratched her head.

'Tropolis chipped its people,' Luca said.

'It's all wrong,' Josetta said unable to stand still. 'I saw a man jump from the fifth floor and smash on the pavement. I even heard gun shots from one of the buildings by the station.' Josetta pushed her rifle onto her back. 'This is madness,' she said as she stared again at the Tropolite people. 'I wanted to keep you safe.'

'She's alive!' Mercy yelled. 'You've got to help her.'

Luca spun round to see Mercy bending over the wild Tropolite. For a moment he did not understand why Mercy would want to help the woman.

'Kelsee,' Mercy called and held out her open hand. 'Your scarf!'

Luca looked at Kelsee who did not move but instead frowned at Mercy.

It took a moment but Kelsee unwrapped it and gave it to Mercy who balled it up and at the woman's shoulder. The Tropolite moaned.

'You've got to get her some help,' she said looking up at Josetta.

Josetta was pale. 'I know where I can go.'

'Take me home,' the woman murmured.

Josetta bent low and lifted the woman who tottered on her feet. She wrapped her arm about the woman's waist. 'I'll get you help.'

'Stop the Outsiders. Protect us!' The woman stuttered.

'I won't be doing that,' Josetta replied. 'The Outsiders and Campion are our only hope.' She held the scarf over the wound.

'The ones that don't have the chip are free from the commands, but they are doing what the Network says,' Eban said.

'I'll find the ones that can listen,' Josetta said holding the woman steady. 'I'll get her help and then find them. Just do your thing quickly, these are my people now and I don't like what is happening to them.'

Josetta passed the woman to one of her crew members who picked her up in his arms. They left the square and merged with the crowd.

The friends went in the opposite direction, with Kelsee confidently leading them towards the contestants' tower.

They had travelled one block closer when Luca held Kelsee back. 'Look!' The Tropolite circle was ordered and neat except for two men that had turned from the group and were cutting across the road. 'There!' Luca pointed.

'Hey!' Eban shouted.

'Shhh!' Luca whispered putting his hand on Eban's chest. 'You were attacked last time, and they are bigger than that woman.' Luca noted how strong they appeared to be.

A third person stepped out from the crowd and she followed the men. She was young and elegant. Soon there were five people walking together but not talking or even acknowledging the others were there. Eban pushed Luca's hand aside and ran towards them, Kelsee was keen to follow but Luca refused to let go of her hand.

Eban walked alongside them for a few paces and Luca could see that he was talking to them, but they gave no sign that they even saw him.

When Eban wandered back he was humming and frowning. He turned to Mercy. 'The command to circle the city is coming from somewhere,' he said. 'But the Network show is saying something else.' He watched the split off group of Tropolites. 'But they are getting a different command. They aren't responding. They have been picked off.'

'There isn't a general command for everyone?' Mercy said. 'Kelsee, do you hear anything different?'

Kelsee frowned a little. 'I don't know,' she replied. 'I feel like I should go to the contestants' building, or near there at least, but that is where we are heading anyway.' Kelsee concentrated for a moment. 'I can't hear *circle the city* anymore.'

Luca looked at the crowds. 'Everyone else does.'

Eban rubbed his chin. 'This means that it isn't just about one command but a network of commands, a multi layered web of commands going out to specific people.' Eban peered up into the sky. The daylight was dimming under the cloud cover. 'These commands are targeting who?'

Mercy shrugged. 'We don't know anyone in Tropolis, so we can't say.'

'Ah!' Eban said his face brighter. 'Tropolis knows who to target because it has a database, it knows the Tropolites and who needs what command. It has picked out that man and that woman. This is run by a computer. Nothing human would be able to organise it to this scale, to have this power.'

Luca had a sudden thought that made his stomach churn. Tropolis power, or at least Hutchings, was targeting certain people. He glanced at Kelsee. She wasn't hearing the general command to circle the city, she was being called to the contestants' building, the location where the ark was hidden and the place where Hutchings was most likely to be. Hutchings was seeking her out. Kelsee had stopped Emundabit, was related to Harland and was a witness to what happened at the mansion. Hutchings was bringing her in to deal with her. Luca shivered. The very place they needed to go was the very place Hutchings was calling Kelsee and was therefore, the very place he wanted Kelsee not to be.

Mercy grabbed Eban's arm. 'We need to stop the signal.'

Eban smiled. 'True, but not that easy.' He took deep breath. 'That signal could be transmitting from any of these buildings, they are tall enough.'

Luca remembered the drones flying over and Kelsee falling to the ground. 'Even if it was from the buildings, it not just them. The drones carry the signal, I expect the Maglev does too. It could be in the pavement for all we know or out in space.' Luca swallowed hard. 'We can't block all the signals.'

Eban laughed. 'We can!' He rubbed his hands together. 'We shut it down at its source.'

'We don't know the source,' Luca said although he had a strong inclination who would be behind it.

'We know that it is a computer and we know that it is reading from a database,' Eban said. 'I can shut down the Network computers.'

'But we need to stop the message that Hutchings altered going out too. You've seen what it does. Tropolis is either being controlled by the computer commands or the footage going out over the Network,' Mercy twiddled the loose strand of hair. 'How can we do both?'

'If I can tap into the main computers, I can do it.'

'We can't. We don't have anything for you to use,' Luca said throwing his hands out in frustration. He wanted to avoid walking into a trap. 'Do you want us to break into a Tropolite home and use theirs?'

Eban smiled, 'That would work!'

'All computers are fingerprint protected,' Kelsee said. 'It would be a waste of precious time.'

'Not all are fingerprint protected,' Mercy said slowly. 'The tablets from the Endurance test training, they were old and we were just handed them.'

'You're right,' Eban said nodding. 'There was no security with them. The training centre is right next to the contestants' building, it is part of the same complex. We are heading there anyway.'

Luca swallowed hard.

'You're forgetting something,' Kelsee said sadly. 'The command is for others to go there too.'

Luca could feel himself tottering and steadied himself before the others noticed.

Chapter 17

The hazy bluish contestants' building stood in the centre of a huge open space. The closest structures were not touched by the building's shadow. The contestants' tower would have stood out against the white and steel façades around it even if it hadn't occupied such an elaborate place in the centre of it all.

Luca hadn't anticipated what he saw when they approached.

The wide space surrounding the building was occupied by armed Tropolites. They were not clad in uniform. These were ordinary people in their Tropolite working clothes equipped with rifles. There were machine guns ready for action with trails of glimmering bullets perched on tripods and rocket lauchers resting on the shoulders of expressionless citizens.

The friends waited at the corner of a neighbouring building.

'Do you think they'd notice us if we just walked in?' Luca asked sarcastically.

It was difficult to gauge from the distance how alert this guard was compared to the circling population.

'We should go in,' Kelsee said in monotone stepping forward.

Luca pulled her back. 'I think Kelsee has given us the answer, or at least Hutchings has.' He touched her face and she blinked rapidly. Did Hutchings know she was here? 'We can't go in this way.' Luca huffed.

'We can go under the tower,' Kelsee said rubbing her temple.

'Is that you or ...'

'That is me thinking,' Kelsee said her face downcast. 'I'm exhausted. The thoughts are so much stronger here and I'm having to fight all the time.'

Luca put his arm around her. 'The Maglev station? How?'

Kelsee shrugged and closed her eyes. 'There is another station nearby, perhaps it has access.'

'Where?'

Kelsee walked slowly away from the tower as if every step were a struggle, but the Maglev station was not far. There were no Tropolites below the city and Kelsee's head seemed to clear a little.

A large map with coloured lines and dots diagrammed the Maglev rails for the city. The station they stood at was marked but the Outside route was nowhere to be seen.

'It's no use, we'll have to go through the guard,' Luca said stamping his foot.

'There are three different Maglev lines that serve this station,' Kelsee said. 'If you look, they avoid this space, the place where the tower is. If we could get to the red platform and onto the track, we could trace it back. There must be way to maintain the rail for Outside.'

'There is only one Maglev that serves that station,' Luca said.

Kelsee frowned at Luca. 'Yes, but it would still need to be worked on occasionally.'

Mercy looked for the red platform signs. 'There is no harm in taking a look. It is at least worth trying,' she said happily.

The platform was completely empty. Its starkness and pristine condition made Luca wonder if the Tropolites ever used the Maglevs. He switched on his torch as they approached the dark tunnel and listened for any sign of an approaching carriage. He licked his lips and wiped his hands on his trousers.

Mercy, who had not been almost crushed by the Maglev showed very little concern. Luca watched Eban, and surprisingly, he too seemed confident that this would be safe.

There was a short ladder at the far end of the platform that led below the Maglev rail. They climbed down. Despite the cleanliness of the Tropolis environment, there was a metallic tang in the air.

Moving away from the edge of the platform and into the darkness, Luca kept close to the wall, keeping the tips of his fingers brushed against the brick surface. It was silent except for their footsteps and the occasional drip of water. Luca felt that every noise he made was amplified and directed down the tunnel announcing their approach. Knowing that the only sounds he heard were theirs was not much of a comfort.

'See!' Kelsee almost shouted. The Maglev rail reached a junction. There were two splits in it where a curved rail came to line up with the main track. 'That way goes to the next station,' Kelsee said. She lifted Luca's torch and pointed it along the curved track.

Luca jumped back and grabbed Kelsee.

The torch beam glistened off the shiny Maglev.

Luca pulled himself close to the wall but a moment later realised that the dark Maglev train sat stationary in the hidden tunnel.

Eban laughed a little from the concrete floor where he had flattened himself and pushed Mercy to the floor. 'Don't do that! I think my heart is going to pound out of my chest.'

When they had recovered from their shock, the friends squeezed past the Maglev, brushing themselves up against the wall. The lower edge of the door was at Luca's eyeline but there was very little room to manoeuvre. Luca was pleased to leave the sleeping machine behind.

This tunnel curved and was much longer than Luca was expecting. He followed the others but was wondering if they should turn back when this service rail met up with another line.

'Which way?' asked Luca.

'I think it is this way,' Kelsee said. 'I want to go, at least I'm being led this way.'

Eban winked. 'It's the one time that we can trust those thoughts to help us out,' Eban whispered.

Luca briefly turned off his torch and listened for voices or any sign that they were discovered. They were alone.

Luca squinted into the darkness. There was a warm spot of light at the other end of the tunnel. He stared at it and suddenly smiled. Luca took a deep breath and brushed down his clothes. He lifted his torch again and they picked their way towards the glow.

Soon there was no need for the torch as the light from the station sparkled off the hundreds of shards of mirrors that lined the walls and curved ceiling. They climbed up the metal ladder and walked along the platform.

Luca stood under the archway and looked up at the multiple reflections of himself and his friends.

He read the familiar sign that stood at the entry to this new world.

WELCOME TO TROPOLIS

He laughed. Maybe it really was time to be welcomed to Tropolis whether the Tropolites knew it or not.

Chapter 18

Luca passed under the arch and began to climb the stairs with Kelsee, Mercy and Eban following closely behind. The flights zigzagged ever higher until at last, the air became cooler and natural light filtered through to them. Kelsee was eager to get to the top but red faced when they stepped from the last landing. They emerged from the relatively enclosed stairwell into the vast open space. The huge windows and steel framework was still as impressive as it had ever been. The marble stone floor gleamed and reflected the high glass ceiling and the sky that was beyond it.

The lobby was empty and quiet. Luca ran to the window to peer down onto the street just one storey below. The Tropolites who had been recruited stood facing out into the city, their backs to the building. Eban tapped Luca and beckoned him to follow. He led them through a door next to the bank of frosted glass doors that had been the cleansing rooms for the Prize contestants.

Luca hesitated. 'The media suite, Eban, is not this way.'

'No, we need to take down the signal first.'

The holding room was still laid out with sofas and a large screen that was blank.

On the far side was the only black door that seemed to exist in Tropolis. The death room was beyond. Luca understood that the death room was a dangerous place to be if you were a failed contestant, but to those that could afford a one to one transfusion, it was a means of life. He shivered at the thought of the pale contestants that he had witnessed when they had found Mercy and Kelsee.

Luca turned away.

Immediately beside them there was a tidy and wide desk. It barred the way to the beautifying area where the Prize contestants had been stripped of their Outsider identities. Luca had been changed so much that he couldn't recognise himself. There was some movement, a shadow was passing in one of the bays and a chinking of bottles.

Luca put his finger to his lips as the others turned towards the sound. A man walked in front of one of the mirrors and Luca caught a flash of a white jacket with royal blue accents. He was a beautifier. Their role in Tropolis was to take the Prize contestants and transform them into candidates that Tropolis would accept. Luca encouraged the others past the desk and was about to follow when the man peered around the edge of a chair obviously hiding on all fours.

'Oh my!' The man stood up suddenly. He was immaculately dressed and accessorised with blue shoes and belt. His stunning hair even had slight glints of deep blue under the artificial light.

Luca gasped. 'Franco?' Luca let out a bark of laughter at seeing his own beautifier.

'Luca, my boy!' Franco whispered rushing up to him. 'And I thought you were gone! How exceptional! How marvellous ... How? How are you here?' Franco peered down his chiselled nose. 'And look at the state of you. What have you been doing?' He tugged on the jumper that Luca was wearing. 'And what is this?'

Luca laughed. 'I'm here and quite alive.' Luca allowed the man to pat him affectionately on the cheek. 'But what about you?'

'Have you seen the program? Outsiders are coming to get us.' Franco put his hand in his pocket and the glass chinked. 'But it looks like you have been dressed by an old woman.'

'So, you thought?'

'About what?

'About the Outsiders coming?'

'Oh, I knew it would happen one day.'

Luca stood back from him. 'What do you mean?'

'I don't know, Luca. I just thought that at some point they would all arrive,' Franco said waving his arms about.

'And you aren't arming yourself or going to march around the city or anything?'

'Arm myself?' Franco asked raising his eyebrows so high they almost got lost in his neat hairline. 'Why would I need to do that?' He patted his pockets and the glass tinkled again. 'Unless you mean arm yourself with some of this excellent cream.' Franco winked and smirked. 'Just a bit of gleaning, that's all.'

'Aren't you worried?' Mercy said.

'Worried of Outsiders? I used to be one.' Franco flashed his wrist and the raised chip implanted there. 'I think I will be fine if the Outsiders invade, and if Tropolis stops them, I am a beautifier, so they will still need me for more Prize competitions.' Franco opened his hands. 'I think I am in a win, win situation.'

Eban grunted.

'Franco,' Luca said carefully. 'Outside don't want to take over, they want to help cure the people of Tropolis.'

Franco giggled. 'So why is Harland Barret still going on and on? Oh, I think he is very worried and it doesn't help that he keeps interrupting all the best programs telling everyone to stay inside and protect themselves. Has anyone told him that Outside want to help?' Franco pulled a small tube of ointment from the table and squeezed a dollop onto his hand. He rubbed the cream in. 'Harland is getting in a right twist, saying he is doing all he can to protect the city, but have you looked out there. All those Tropolites and they are not listening to him. What's he doing? I mean, I haven't seen any sign of trouble have you?' Franco sniffed at his palms. 'Mmm, lovely.' He looked up at Luca. 'I don't know that Outside will come to Tropolis. I think that they will just go away – after all, Tropolis didn't welcome them with open arms and hasn't really had much to do with them has it?'

Luca shrugged. 'Tropolis hasn't done much to help, no.'

'Except make you and your friends look so much better,' Franco said smiling and sweeping his hand across to point to them all.

'Outside and others are coming,' Mercy said.

'I hope that they do,' Franco replied flicking Mercy's loose strand of hair out of the way. 'I have so many friends who are so very ill. They would dearly love to walk away from the fatigue. You know, I often go to their houses and give them a bit of a lift with some beauty treatments. There have to be a few perks to this job, eh? They are always so much better afterwards.'

Luca nodded. 'That's right. They would be better.' Luca thought that Franco's kindness had been the exact medicine that they really needed. 'You have been doing a great job.'

Franco tilted his head. 'Ah! I knew I liked you.'

Luca leaned closer. 'I think that the leaders of Tropolis don't want the people to get better.'

Franco stood wide eyed and covered his mouth. 'No!'

'It's true,' Kelsee said from behind Eban.

'Kelsee Barret!' Franco exclaimed. 'I've always wanted to meet you. Oh, I have the most amazing product that would do miraculous things with your hair.'

'Great!' Kelsee said sarcastically. 'Only, right now we are doing something a bit more important.'

'Nothing is more important than good hair!'

Luca shook his head. 'Except maybe ensuring that Tropolis gets a cure.'

'Yes, yes!' Franco nodded. 'Yes, quite right.' He stepped to one side and spoke to Kelsee. 'I could pop a little in it now. It won't take long.'

'Not right now, thank you.'

'I love good manners,' Franco said beaming at Kelsee. 'Perhaps I can help you in another way.'

Kelsee wrinkled her nose.

'You mustn't do that,' Franco said smoothing his own flawless skin with his fingers. 'You'll create lines, undo all the good work of the lotions.'

'Actually Franco,' Luca said. 'I think you can help.' He pointed to the door opposite with the control pad entry. 'Can you open that door?'

'Oh yes,' Franco said. 'I have access to all the places my charges may need me.'

'You can get us into the Endurance training centre?'

'I can!'

Franco strutted over to the door and scanned the panel with his wrist. The lever clicked; the heavy double glass doors slid open. 'Easy!'

Eban laughed and patted Franco on the back as he dashed past.

They hurried along the bridge-like corridor that gave a view into Tropolis, but Luca stayed focused on doors at the other end.

'Oh dear!' Franco began.

'What?' asked Luca.

'Do you know that you have disgusting dark smears all over your back?' Franco said trying to brush them off.

Luca blinked for a long second and took a steadying breath. 'White is not a very practical colour to wear,' he replied trying to keep the sarcasm out of his voice.

'It takes time to know how to handle it,' Franco said as he scanned the second set of doors and they unlocked.

The raised mezzanine was at eye level with the high windows that provided the gentle natural light for the training room below. There was no barrier to stop people falling. Luca peered over the edge. The net was still in place and it was the quickest way down.

Franco stood next to him. 'Will you be here for long?' he asked.

Luca watched as Eban launched himself off the side and landed in the net below. 'I don't know,' he said.

'Well,' Franco said, carefully stepping away from the drop. 'If you don't need me anymore.'

'Thank you!' Luca smiled. He stood so that his back was to the edge. 'You have been really helpful.'

Franco reached for the door and turned to wave. Luca laughed as he saw the look of horror in Franco's wide eyes as he let himself fall backwards over the edge. The sensation lasted only a matter of seconds, but the thrill energized him.

The huge white room was arranged with the various apparatus that Luca was very familiar with. The ropes, frames and ladders, balance beams and climbing nets were not as frightening to him now. He had mastered a few of the skills and had endured the bruises from the mistakes he had made and the lack of crash mats. Although the lotions that Franco was so keen on did accelerate the healing process dramatically.

Luca called to Kelsee. She peered down at him and looked pale. Mercy took her away from the edge. Moments later they appeared at the far side of the mezzanine where the scramble net was fixed. She climbed down, Mercy helping her with the method.

'Cheat!' Luca said gently punching Mercy's shoulder.

She shook her head and pranced past him.

They skirted the training gear and walked through the archway at the far side of the room. The pool was completely still and the water mirror-like. A lazy steam rose from its surface.

Eban reached for the only door to see that it was locked.

'Franco?' Eban asked, his voice echoing strangely.

'I didn't think we'd need him again,' Luca said. 'Sorry.'

Eban waved his hand. 'Not to worry.' He jammed open the scanner box with the clip on the radio and began pulling out the wires.

Luca dipped his fingers in the water sending ripples over the surface and magical swirls of light over the ceiling. Grime from the journey dripped from his hand and temporarily stained the water before it dissolved away. He rubbed both hands together and washed them clean then dried them on his trousers.

The sudden distinct click of the lock being released made Luca smile once again. He turned and Eban had pushed open the door.

Four long and narrow shooting alleys stretched out with fresh, brightly coloured targets in the distance. Ear defenders and a variety of guns hung from hooks next to each alley. Luca frowned at the weapons. He recoiled. Luca could not understand how this had been the place that Thickset had been attracted to.

To one side was a tall counter. Eban slid over the polished surface and began to search behind. Luca dashed around the end and joined him. He pushed things aside and they bumped and scraped the shelves. There were several opened small boxes of red and blue cartridges of different sizes. Eban moved them away. He leaned in and pulled on a scruffy cardboard box and then lifted it to the counter top. He opened it, reached in and smiled.

He lifted out a handful of canvas covered tablets. They were battered and dirty, but Luca laughed at the possibility of actually succeeding at something.

Eban pressed the small round button in the corner. The screen lit up.

The artificial light made Eban's eyes shine. He looked up at the others and winked. 'It's time to shut the signal down.'

Chapter 19

Eban had arranged a number of tablets around him; each screen glowed a different colour. He sat in the corner, picking up one tablet at a time, swiping the screen, tapping at it and typing in code. He was focused and non-verbal.

Luca didn't know what to do with himself. They hadn't stopped for hours and now they were just waiting. He strolled around the training room, almost tempted to climb the rope or walk the beam to rid himself of the nervous energy. He knew that the only thing that would satisfy him would be to get to the media suite and play that video footage.

He considered suggesting that they split up, that Kelsee stay here and he and Mercy go to the video room. Luca knew it wasn't worth discussing as he would have no idea what to do to get it broadcast. He was reliant on Eban.

He paced the perimeter of the pool then collected a couple of the opened boxes from behind the counter. Luca tossed a red canister into the water with a musical plop. He smirked and tossed another, enjoying the gurgling noise. There was a silvery blue fish design in the middle of the swimming pool that seemed to make as good a target as any. Luca began to throw the bullets into the water, aiming for the fish. It took several goes before he had worked out how the water affected the way the cartridges sank. Soon even that become tedious.

Kelsee cleared her throat as if she were irritated. 'What are we going to do when he is done?' she asked. 'How much longer will it take?'

Luca sighed.

'I am here you know,' Eban said without looking at them.

Everyone was silent once more. Luca sat propped up against the wall and leaned his head back. He watched the shadows lengthen and the colour of the late evening light warm the brilliant white walls.

Eban thumped the floor and yelled in frustration.

Kelsee turned. 'Have you managed to get into the main Network computers?'

'No,' Eban replied sharply. 'I can't get around the defences.'

Luca let his gaze drop. He knew that Hutchings had formed the perfect solution to invasion or any sign of overthrowing power. She could control the people of Tropolis. It had been a plan formed over many years and it was no wonder that Eban couldn't break through.

'What now then?' Luca asked. 'It's no use playing the video message without the people being able to see it and hear it and we can't get Outside and Campion to come in, the Tropolites could turn at any moment. They'll be destroyed.'

'I have another idea, but you might not like it,' Eban said.

'I might not?' Luca said.

'I don't think anyone will like it.'

Luca opened his hands. 'Let's hear it,' he said. 'It's got to be better than doing nothing.'

Eban sighed. 'I've been trying to break through walls on the system but there is no way in. If I were in, I could make just a tiny crack and then the whole lot would come down.'

'But you aren't in,' Mercy clarified. 'You just told us that.'

'There is a possibility of getting something to their side,' Eban stated. 'A virus.' Eban lifted a tablet and circled it with his finger. 'I can put together a simple code and it won't even be noticed until it is too late.'

Luca scowled at Eban. 'Then do it. What not to like about that?'

'What are you planning?' Kelsee said with interest.

'I need them,' Eban said as he pointed to the centre of the tablet. He then scooped the air from the edge of the tablet into its middle. 'To take it in.' Eban then half smiled. 'I need bait.' He waited a moment then added. 'It would be even better if the woman herself took it in because she will be right at the centre.'

Luca frowned. 'You want Hutchings to start a virus in her computer?'

'I want her to introduce the virus. Correct.'

Luca looked back at the shadows. 'She won't do that.'

'Bait?' Kelsee asked. 'What bait?'

'You,' Eban replied confidently.

Luca faced Eban. 'No!'

'Eban!' Mercy scolded.

'Why not?' Kelsee asked looking at them.

'You've seen what she has done with her bait.'

'Let's hear the full plan,' Kelsee said. 'Eban?'

Luca glared at Eban, but it didn't stop him.

'She asked,' Eban said. 'I create a virus. I hide it in a file and send it to Hutchings.'

'And Kelsee is involved how?' Luca pushed.

'The message will come from Kelsee.' Eban scratched his chin.

'I could tell her I want revenge for what she has done,' Kelsee suggested.

'You could,' Eban agreed. 'Only the revenge would be the virus.'

Eban got to his feet and tipped all the tablets over the counter. He sorted through them turning each of them over in his hand. He picked one and switched it on.

'We could record a message,' Eban said pointing at the tiny camera lens. 'Show her that you are in Tropolis and that you are coming after her.'

'Eban!' Mercy protested.

'It would be just to get her to play the video. I can hide the virus in the video and she would have no idea that I got in.'

'I am in theory coming after her,' Kelsee said calmly.

'Hey!' Luca said raising his voice. 'If she knows you are here, she *will* come after you.' Luca touched his forehead with his fingers. 'This is too dangerous. She knows that you have all the information you need about Emundabit and she knows you stopped it. She would have killed you before now if she only knew where to find you. You can't tell her.' Luca put his arm in front of Kelsee. 'This is what Hutchings wants.'

'Then this is the best plan,' Kelsee said.

Luca growled. 'Please Kelsee,' he begged.

Kelsee smiled peacefully. 'You know, since you made me aware that my thoughts were actually their thoughts, I've known that she wants me dead. Hutchings has an even bigger plan than Emundabit. If she was able to convince the board to agree to destroying people who weren't part of the city, do you think she would stop there?'

Mercy sighed. 'I think you are right. I think she intends to re-create Tropolis with herself as the glorious leader.' Mercy gazed at Luca. 'You are such a different person to the one that left Outside. You care about people. You allowed yourself to really care.'

'I care about Kelsee.' Luca pulled her close. 'Mercy, you have to know that.'

Mercy smiled. 'I know that.'

'Do you remember when Mercy was taken to the death room?' Eban asked.

Luca's eyes began to moisten. 'I can't do that again.'

'But you thought,' Eban said, and then corrected himself, 'I should say both of us thought that Mercy really was gone, but look, she is not only here but was able to save Kelsee by choosing to walk through that door.'

'That was my fault too,' Luca whispered.

'I want to do this,' Kelsee said quietly. 'This isn't about just me or you, this is about all those people out there circling the city or defending this building. My little bit might be the thing that gives them freedom.'

'I can't keep you safe,' Luca admitted. He hung his head. 'If you walk through this door, you will be her target.'

'If I walk through this door, I think we can change it all.' Kelsee laughed. 'Don't you see? Don't you understand the trap we can lay? All those thoughts to harm you, to destroy you, then the call to the city and the call to come to this building. She planted those thoughts, she will think she has already won. If I have given in to her demands to get here, why wouldn't I have killed you too? She doesn't need to know that you are with me.'

'She under estimates you!' Eban said confidently.

'Yes, she does,' replied Kelsee. 'And if she thinks that she only has me to deal with she won't see the attack coming from you.'

'And we could stop her before Kelsee gets into danger?' asked Luca.

'That's the plan.'

Luca slowly nodded. 'Alright. We'll do it.' Luca caught the flash of a smile from Kelsee. 'But the video needs to have nothing in it to show where Kelsee is.'

'And I'll film it myself so she thinks I'm alone.'

Eban handed her the tablet with the camera. 'It'll need to capture her attention and make her watch to the end. I'll get working on that virus.'

Luca watched Kelsee as she scribbled some ideas on another screen. She muttered to herself, pulling faces and giggling at random moments.

The light was almost gone when she announced that she was ready to film. Eban was surrounded by the glowing lights of the tablets that he was working on, so Kelsee took herself out to the far corner of the training room. She made Luca stay with Eban and began to film.

A few minutes later Kelsee came back. Her eyes were red as if she'd been crying but she was beaming with excitement.

'Do you want to see it?'

Kelsee placed the tablet into Luca's hands. She pressed the play icon and then tutted. 'Oh no! There's no sound.'

Luca shook his head. 'There is,' he said. 'My chip is letting me hear it.' Kelsee sat down next to him and rested her chin on his shoulder while he watched.

The camera angle was low and Kelsee's features appeared strange being illuminated by the tablet's light. 'Mara Hutchings. I want to talk to you,' she began. 'I don't like you and that's no lie. You killed my grandfather and I have evidence.' Kelsee turned away from the screen as if she were looking around her. 'Murder is a terrible thing. You planned it, you wanted him dead.' She paused and stared into the camera but was distant somehow. 'I've killed now. I don't know how that happened.' Tears rolled down her cheeks. 'I know you won't care about him, but Luca was my friend,' Kelsee paused and looked confused. 'I thought he was my friend. But I knew he was going to hurt me. It was self-defence.' Kelsee focused back on the camera and sniffed. 'But what you did, what you did!' Kelsee said pointing an accusing finger, 'You killed my grandfather. He was an old and weak man. He had been left in his mansion for years. You may have fooled Tropolis that he still leads, but I know the truth. I know the truth and I am coming to get you!' Kelsee sneered. 'I know where your office is in this building and I am coming to get you.' Kelsee lowered her voice into a menacing hiss. 'Wherever you hide I will find you. I've already killed once, and I know I can do it again because I know what you have done.' The screen went dark.

Luca blinked.

'What do you think?' Kelsee asked innocently.

'You are very scary.'

'I am?' Kelsee laughed. 'I knew all those acting lessons would be worth it.' She lifted the tablet from Luca's hands and slid it in front of Eban. 'All done!'

Eban broke from what he had been doing and watched the video. Luca laughed nervously at the wide-eyed expression on Eban's face.

He looked up at her. 'Wow! I think that will capture her attention.' He slid the video off the screen and it appeared on one of the ones on the floor next to him. 'Do you have a messaging system?'

Kelsee nodded.

'I need you to sign in.' Eban handed her a different tablet.

Mercy and Luca watched. The four of them were huddled in the corner of the shooting range. The only light came from the tablets scattered on the floor. Mercy and Luca had their backs to the wall and Kelsee crawled over to pass a screen to him.

'I've found her messaging address for her office, but I suspect that she monitors and manages your grandfather's account too,' Eban said. Kelsee closed her lips tightly and her nostrils flared. 'I'll send the message to both those places.'

'Then we just wait.'

'I don't think it will be long before she watches it.' Eban looked up at Luca. There was a green glow in the room. 'Shall I do this?' he asked.

They all nodded. Eban tapped the screen and the snare was set.

'Do what?' the crisp voice echoed over the water.

Everyone jolted and turned. Kelsee screamed at the man that stood in the doorway.

Chapter 20

'What are you going to do and what are you doing here?' the man demanded. He had something over his arm.

Kelsee tried to back away. 'Don't hurt us!' she pleaded.

Luca squinted into the darkness. 'Alec?'

'When Franco said you were here ...'

'That is you isn't it Alec?' Luca said unsure.

'Of course.' Alec threw down a pile of white fabric. 'Franco came into the Prize supply rooms to get you clothes. Why?'

'I think he wanted us to look good,' Eban said.

'Not why do you need clothes,' Alec said angrily. 'Why are you here?' He bent down. The dim light could not disguise his pained expression or his furrowed brow.

'We sent you a message,' Luca said. 'The tower contacted you.'

'I've had no contact with anyone,' Alec replied. 'I was able to warn Campion but was disturbed so had to go into hiding. When I was able to I came looking for you, but you were gone from the place we agreed.' Alec puffed out a long breath.

'You didn't send the Maglev?'

Alec shook his head. 'What Maglev? I didn't know where you were.'

Mercy put her hand on her forehead. 'They sent it. You were right, Luca.'

Alec's expression softened. 'When you weren't where I told you to be I thought you had been caught and were dead.'

Luca glanced away. 'I'm sorry,' he said. 'We had to do something to stop Tropolis from attacking. Kelsee wanted to confront her grandfather, tell him about the real lives he was affecting.'

'You went to Harland Barret?' Alec exclaimed. 'Are you mad?'

Luca leaned towards his uncle. 'Harland was an old man. He was trapped in his mansion. He hasn't set foot in Tropolis for years.'

Alec tilted his head to one side. 'That would make sense. He's never available to speak to in person. It is always via the Network.'

Kelsee sighed. 'I doubt you ever spoke to him.'

'Hutchings is behind it all,' Luca stated. 'She somehow uses Harland's image and is able to hide inside it. She is ultimately in power.'

'I had thought it strange,' Alec said, 'But I rarely spoke with him. It was usually through Hutchings.' Alec shook his head, trying to put things in order. 'Since I came back from Outside and she wanted me sent back on that Maglev, I've kept my distance. I don't know who to trust and I thought that if Mara Hutchings knew I was here she would dispose of me. She's made that very clear.'

Luca put his hand on Kelsee's leg. 'She came to the mansion and accelerated Emundabit, but we stopped it with the help of Harland who died in the process.'

'I don't think you've stopped it,' Alec said. 'I've seen the drones flying out and the city is behaving strangely.'

'This is different,' Eban said. 'Hutchings has set Tropolis, Outside and Campion up. She knows about all of them and is planning something else. Have you seen the footage from Outside?'

'Of course,' Alec replied. 'It is about time Tropolis got invaded. I'm glad that the army I sent in have joined forces with Outside.'

'You saw her editing it,' Luca said frowning. 'How could you believe it?'

'That's not what is happening,' Mercy said. 'Campion also came to Outside to help. They wanted to bring that long awaited freedom to the Outsiders. But now they are working together. We sent the message to Tropolis, but Hutchings changed it. Outside and Campion are coming to rescue Tropolis; to set them free from the fatigue.'

'Why would they do that? Tropolis has lied, stolen and killed them.'

Mercy nodded. 'All true, but Tropolis is made up of people too. People who have families, friends and lives. Outside and Campion have come to realise that Tropolites are suffering in a different way.'

Alec took a deep breath. 'Tropolis power has been destroying lives for years. I've tried to rebel in my own small way, doing what I can when I could. What can we do? This is too big.'

'Firstly,' Eban replied, not rising to the despair in Alec's tone, 'We wake the people of Tropolis up. We change what they hear and what they see.'

Alec glanced at each of the friends' faces. 'And how do we do that?'

'The media suite,' Luca replied.

Alec helped Luca from the ground. 'Then let's go.'

Eban grabbed two of the tablets and held them awkwardly as he climbed up the scramble net in the near darkness that crept over the city. When Alec opened the door to the bridge, the sudden movement turned on the automatic lighting system and the bright light shocked Luca. Alec had refused to turn on any of the lights in the training room to not draw attention to themselves. Luca began to run. They needed to act fast, before they were discovered. Alec rushed to let them into the holding room and then into the lobby beyond.

Luca didn't even notice the atrium as he sprinted to the far side and waited. He put his hand against the sensor. The red light flashed down his palm. Nothing happened.

'I don't have access,' Luca said and bit on his lip. 'Only Alec does.'

Kelsee put her hand against the square, but even she didn't have admission.

'Let me,' Alec said moving them aside. 'They already know I am here.'

A loud thud from behind him caught Luca's attention.

Luca approached the tall windows that looked out towards the city. There were no lights shining from the buildings and the streets were only lit by the fading twilight sky. Lights out was in place over every other building in Tropolis. Luca peered down.

A white clad woman stood on the other side of the glass wall. She was staring inside the lower atrium, thumping the glass and shouting something. Soon another person had joined her. A couple of men had picked up a canister of some kind and began to bang it against the glass. They were pale. The bright glow from the contestants' building had not attracted any attention from the puppet people of Tropolis.

'She knows we're here!' Luca shouted. 'A new command has been given.'

'This way!' called Eban.

Luca turned and saw the open door. Bright light filled the corridor. The power was still running in this building. Luca knew that the ark had everything to do with this fact.

Luca pointed and ran to the end of the corridor. He pushed the button to call the lift then pushed open the door to the stairwell. Luca listened but there was no sound of anyone coming for them rising from the basement and the ark deep below the city.

A loud smash echoed in the atrium and then the sudden noise of shouting flowed down the corridor.

The lift doors opened, and the friends hurried in seeking the sanctuary. Luca punched the Media suite button, the doors shut and the violence was silenced.

Luca's stomach lurched a little as the lift rose. Eban checked his tablet and laughed at Luca's hopeful expression.

'I've got a bite,' he replied.

'She's let you in?' asked Kelsee. 'So why am I desperately wanting to go down instead of up.'

'Hutchings couldn't resist you!' Eban said. 'And now she is calling you to where she wants you.'

The lift doors opened lazily.

Bright spot lights shone on the floor of the Media suite. Luca had, at first, been startled by the faces looking back at him when the doors opened. The static images of the icons of Tropolis that decorated the walls were larger than life but Eban couldn't help himself from laughing at Luca's reaction.

Kelsee hung back. She held her side and looked wide eyed at the familiar corridor. Luca reached out to her and offered his hand. When she took it, he could feel her shaking. 'We're safe here. Hutchings will be in the ark, I'm certain of it.'

Luca advanced up the corridor with confidence, no longer hiding in the shadows. He peered through the glass panel of the door before he entered. All the monitors were blank.

'Excellent!' exclaimed Eban rushing forward and switching the screens on.

'I'll check the other rooms,' Alec said walking away.

'They were doing stuff to your message on this screen,' Luca said releasing Kelsee and leaning forward to flick a switch. There was only the blank white room on the screen now. 'But they were twisting these and tapping stuff over here.'

Mercy had gone deeper into the room and was turning on all the switches she could find.

Eban pulled a chair over to the section where Luca stood and began to examine the controls.

'Is this the control room for the Network broadcasts?' Mercy asked as she walked to the far side of the bank of monitors. 'It seems so small to do so much damage.'

The white room on the screen flipped to a still shot of Eban.

'Now, there's a handsome fella!' Eban said joyfully. Luca watched as Eban twisted a dial and the film rewound rapidly. 'Now to transfer it over to the Network.'

A sudden high-pitched shriek made Luca turn quickly.

Kelsee had a gun pointed at her head and her arm twisted behind her back. The uniform clad Atticus smiled maliciously.

Chapter 21

'Stop right there!' he ordered harshly as he lifted Kelsee's arm higher. She winced. 'I don't think you should be in here.' Atticus was dishevelled and dirty. His face was smeared with soot or oil and his uniform was stained.

'Leave her alone!' Luca demanded.

'I don't take my orders from you.'

'No,' Luca snapped, 'You take them from Hutchings.'

Atticus laughed. 'That I do!'

Mercy stepped away from the monitors and faced Atticus. 'Did you think you would find her here?'

'She'll be here somewhere and when she sees that I have you lot she will be very pleased with me.'

Luca shook his head. 'But she isn't here, Sergeant. She is in the ark.' Luca tried to look innocent but couldn't help but feel a surge of power over this vicious man. 'Did you not get the invite?' Luca pushed his lips together faking disappointment. 'Perhaps it was mislaid,' Luca said with wide eyes, 'or she didn't want you to be saved either.'

'Of course I know about the ark. I wasn't aware that was already happening as I've been busy elsewhere. But don't doubt that I am a valued and highly esteemed member of Tropolis,' Atticus defended.

The door opened behind Atticus. He took a sudden intake of breath and jumped forward.

'I wouldn't put it quite like that!' Alec also held a weapon, but it didn't look as easy in his hand. 'Leave the girl alone,' he ordered.

Atticus slowly lowered his gun and let Kelsee go, pushing her roughly to the side. 'You!' he spat. 'It's your fault that Tropolis is in uproar. You sent those troops to Outside. Traitor!' he hissed.

'The only treacherous thing I have done is not act sooner.' Alec motioned to Atticus. 'Drop your weapon.'

The sergeant gently placed the gun on the floor and then kicked it towards the door. 'I'm not surprised you didn't get a place in the ark. She wanted you dead.'

'She wanted a lot of things. But Tropolis is not going to be hers. I only came back to get that message out.' Alec relaxed his stance a little. 'Eban, can you broadcast it over the Network?'

Luca shrugged. 'The power is down over Tropolis.'

'There is still one screen functioning,' Alec stated, 'The one in the lobby.' He nodded. 'Can you set the volume high? The people have broken in and are currently in the building. The word will spread if we can get them to just stop and see it.'

'They won't hear it until the signal is shut down,' Luca said.

'I'll set it to play in a loop,' Eban said. 'As soon as the power is back on, it will play on every Network screen there is.'

Atticus huffed in the corner but didn't appear to be bothered by Alec's gun that still pointed at him.

Eban began to fiddle with the tablets placing them on the small desk space in front of him.

Luca watched the screen and at long last listened to the message that had been his mission to restore.

'Greetings from Outside!' Eban's face was friendly and he was smiling widely. 'I am Eban, an Outsider and Compassion Prize contestant. As you can see there are quite a few of us here.' The camera panned the area. It was a wide shot taken by the docks in

Outside. The images weren't through the fencing but were by the water side. A huge barge laden with waste was moored, a refuse moving truck was holding the fence down and thousands of people were crowded in the once restricted area. Some were in smaller groups and talking to each other intently, others were just flocking to an area that had been off limits for too long. Luca had never stood where his people were standing. He smiled.

The shot then focused back on Eban. He had turned the camera back to himself and started to chat to the viewers. 'I know that this may not be what you are used to seeing, but this is Outside. These people are real and have a tough existence. For many years,' Eban continued with a serious expression, 'Tropolis have treated Outside wrongfully.' Eban shook his fist. 'The powers of Tropolis have hidden what they have done to this people and lived on the stolen souls of a people group it has tried to crush.' Eban repositioned himself. 'Things are difficult here.' He panned the shot so that the distant heaps could be seen and even some of the shacks. His voice came over the footage. 'These are our homes and this is our lot in life because we were born in Outside.' He turned the camera back to himself. 'The power and strength of Tropolis have made us what we are. They like to think of us as less than human. You would be right to think that we live off what you throw away, but we have discovered something that you need.' Eban smiled into the camera. 'We used to think that we were good for nothing but all that has changed.' Eban smiled at the camera. 'We have heard of your plight. We have been told of the fatigue. We know that you are human too and we want to help.' Eban nodded into the camera and grinned. 'We believe we have the cure.'

Eban sighed. 'Our world has suddenly become much bigger. We have been found by a group called Campion, they are neither Outsider nor Tropolite, but they will be bringing us to you. We want you to be confident and not concerned that we are angry and want revenge. That is far from our minds. We know that you are suffering, we understand what it is to suffer. We have the answer.

Look at this people, the mix of Campion and Outsider, you can see, the people here are united.' Eban once again panned the camera over the crowd. When he came into shot he had a few instructions. 'You will need to arrange for transfusion supplies and to sort the people into blood type groups. You are to bring out those that are sickest first, since we want to treat them before anyone else. We want the whole population of Tropolis to be healthy, starting with the weakest.' Eban squinted as the sun broke through. 'We are not asking for anything in return. We want to extend a hand of friendship and not of conflict. We want you to live. Get ready! We are coming!'

The screen went black for a moment and then the message played again.

'You've done it, Eban,' Luca said. 'Tropolis can now see it.'

'Once the power comes on,' Eban said. 'In the meantime ...'

Luca was distracted by a sudden movement in the peripheral of his vision.

Thickset burst into the room. 'In the meantime, put that gun down,' he demanded.

'I'll do no such thing,' Alec said.

'You took your time!' Atticus accused. 'Shoot the idiot!' Thickset stared at Alec and then at Atticus. 'Just do it!'

Thickset swallowed hard.

'You don't have to do this Seth,' Mercy said kindly.

'Leave me alone!'

'We can't leave you alone whilst you hold that gun to Alec,' Luca said. 'Just put it down.'

Thickset turned to Luca but kept the rifle touching Alec's back. 'What's it to you if I shoot him?'

'He hasn't done anything to you,' Luca stated.

Thickset scowled. 'I'm here.'

'But that wasn't his fault.'

'Shoot him!' Atticus demanded.

Mercy stepped forward. 'I saw what happened in the settlement, in the library,' she said gently. 'That isn't who you are.'

'You didn't see anything.'

'You shot Debs,' Luca whispered loud enough for everyone to hear.

Thickset glanced at Atticus. 'He shot her, not me.' Thickset's voice wobbled a little.

'That's right,' Mercy agreed. 'You were going to let her live.'

Seth turned to her. 'How do you know that?'

Mercy took another step forward. 'I think you are regretting choosing Tropolis over Outside.'

'Shoot him, then kill her!' Atticus spat.

'Shut up!' Thickset shouted. 'Let me think.'

Luca had, possibly for the first time since he had met Thickset, a small measure of admiration for him.

Atticus attempted to move but Alec jabbed him with his weapon.

'It isn't complicated, boy!' Atticus shouted. 'Kill the lot of them or let me do it if you aren't man enough.'

'Seth is man enough, but you have a twisted idea of what a man is,' Mercy replied. 'Being man enough is walking away from doing what is wrong.'

'I'm not wrong!' Atticus yelled. 'You should have died in the death room, in fact you should have died a lot earlier. Tropolis doesn't need Outside trash like you.'

'You are wrong. I'm exactly the type of trash Tropolis really needs.'

'Hutchings wouldn't think so.' Atticus glared at Thickset. 'Are you going to do this or not? If you want to be one of the chosen you must do this. I won't take you otherwise.'

Mercy glared at Atticus then looked kindly at Seth. 'If you give into him now, he'll only demand it again and again of you. I'm not sure that is the type of chosen I'd want to be,' she said. 'You have to stand up to him.'

Thickset glanced at Luca. 'What are you staring at?'

'I wasn't,' Luca replied. 'Seth, Mercy is right.'

'Why should I trust you?'

'I don't know, but letting Atticus bully you into killing someone doesn't sound like what a leader should be. I know you want something better than that.' Luca tried to smile at Seth. He wanted to look past all the stuff that he had been subject to at this person's hands. He remembered what had been said earlier about the control of Tropolis and how Thickset was trapped in that control. He needed an escape route. 'You are better than that,' Luca said with conviction, choosing to see the glowing ember of goodness that had suddenly flared to life for Seth. It had ignited his own compassion for him. 'Don't you want to follow someone who leads because of who they are and not because of what will happen to you if you fail to obey?'

Everyone relaxed as they watched as Seth's rifle butt lowered. Atticus swiped Alec's weapon from his hand and reached for his own gun laying by the door. As Atticus lifted it and prepared to fire, Seth stepped to one side so that he was blocking Luca, turned and aimed. Before Seth had a chance to consider what he was going to do, he pulled the trigger. Attius must have fired a moment after because both fell to the ground.

Alec pulled the rifle from Atticus' limp hand, pushed his weapon out of arms reach and leaned over the body. He checked for a pulse. There was none.

Luca gave his attention to Seth. It had all happened so fast and Luca was certain that Seth had stepped in front of him and into the path of Atticus' bullet. The bullet that would have hit him if it hadn't hit Seth. He knelt at Seth's side.

Seth's breathing was laboured.

He reached over to Luca and pulled him close. Luca resisted 'You are right,' he said struggling to breathe. He wasn't vicious and threatening.

Luca relaxed and leaned closer. 'About what?'

'We should want to follow a leader.' Seth winced. Blood was pooling through his uniform.

Luca pressed on Seth's wound to try to stem the flow.

'I had it all wrong,' Seth admitted, his eyes shut in pain. 'Wrong about you and about Tropolis.' He briefly looked up into Luca's face. 'I'm sorry for what I did to you.'

Luca held his breath, not knowing what to say or do. Thickset had tried to kill him and outrank him in everything the Compassion Prize contest offered. This young man was not recognisable. He was broken and dying. Luca could have just pushed Thickset aside; he had, after all, deserved all that he had received, but Seth was the unarmed, once hidden and now seen Outsider. Luca knew that he needed to let all that history go before it was too late. 'I forgive you,' he whispered.

'I saw the families in Outside,' Seth said sadly. 'I have none. Just wanted someone. Thought I'd fit here.' He grabbed Luca even tighter and pulled him very close. Luca could feel his struggling breath. 'You have to stop her.' Seth coughed. 'Stop Hutchings.'

'We intend to.'

'She's going to destroy everyone,' Seth said with effort, his gaze fixed on Luca. 'Ark is ... the only ... safe place.'

'Everyone?' asked Kelsee.

Seth nodded. 'Tropolis not free. In danger too.'

Luca placed his hand on Seth's head; the short hair prickly under his fingers. 'We are going to do all that we can to make sure that she doesn't succeed. Tropolis, Outside and Campion; they all need to be free.'

Seth's grip was weakening. 'If I could do it again,' he said his voice barely a whisper. 'I would follow you and your friends.'

Luca knelt wide eyed at the statement. 'You took that bullet for me, didn't you?'

Seth smiled, closed his eyes and died. He looked as if he was sleeping, pain no longer etched in his features but peaceful at the last moment.

Luca sighed. The glowing ember of goodness he had chosen to see in Thickset had been become a fiery furnace in Seth. His enemy had been conquered, but not at his hands; it was a change of heart that had won.

He wiped his blood-drenched hand on his white jumper. 'Franco will be furious!' he said under his breath.

Luca stood and watched a couple of seconds of the message from Outside. It was still running as if nothing had happened in this tiny control room, but Luca felt the magnitude of what had occurred.

Mercy put her arm around him. 'Some people make the best choices right at the very end.'

'He died because of me,' Luca said frowning.

'Yes,' Mercy replied softly. 'But you still don't understand how others see you.'

'I'm not worth taking a bullet for,' Luca replied. 'And even less worth following.'

'Do you know what you have done and are about to do?

Luca rubbed his hands against the fabric in his sleeve. 'I've watched you and Eban and Kelsee,' he said, and they turned towards him. He gestured to Mercy. 'You've taken the blame, given blood, saved lives.' He took Kelsee's hand. 'Confronted the enemy and seen the truth.' He turned to Eban 'Motivated Outside and Campion, rescued the video message and started a virus in the Network.' He shrugged whilst he spoke. 'I've just come along for the ride.'

'Stop that!' Eban said. 'You really can't see it can you?'

'See what?'

'You have been able to change lives,' Kelsee said. Luca raised his eyebrows questioning her theory and shook his head. 'Mine!'

'Willow and Amil,' Mercy said.

'Mine too,' said Alec. 'I'm grateful that I can come out of hiding.'

'Harland Barret and now Seth,' Mercy said.

'They died.'

'Yes, but you set them free,' Mercy stated. 'You didn't have to do that.'

'I know what it would be like to not free them. I've been there. Living with bitterness or revenge is only damaging yourself. It was selfish in the end.'

'What you have done is like those old stories of myth,' Kelsee said gripping his hand tightly. 'The dead would be floated on a boat out on a lake and then set alight. The fire became a way or a door into the afterlife.' Kelsee smiled at Luca. 'It is as if you were able to strike the match to light the fire and let them go. You haven't just shown them the door but opened it for them too.'

'I think they call that compassion, Luca,' Eban said smiling. 'Only when you do it, it's like a compassion fire, burning brighter in you each and every day.'

'It takes courage to let them go,' Mercy said. 'Don't underestimate what you do, who you are or what you are capable of.'

Luca was silent. He had not thought that his tiny contribution could have made such a difference. He bit down on his tongue to distract the tears from forming.

Eban picked up the tablet and swiped the screen. A small video icon appeared on the screen. Eban tapped on it and the recorded video began to play at a different rate to the one over the Network. 'I think it is worth saving this here. I don't want to lose it again.'

'Eban,' Kelsee said, leaning away from Luca. 'I think you have infected the system. I'm thinking clearly again, in fact clearer than I have for ages.'

He laughed. 'And you have a new, personal message, Kelsee.'

Kelsee wiped her hands against her clothes and reached for the tablet. 'Hutchings by any chance?'

Luca read over her shoulder.

Dear Kelsee,

I have received your garbled threat and would warn you that I have the best legal defence that Tropolis can offer. You should be very careful about slandering someone without evidence of the truth. I, however, have saved your enlightening revelations of guilt in the partaking of murder.

I suggest that you come to meet me, perhaps I can assist you and provide the medical help that you require.

If you are in Tropolis, you will be able to find me in the contestants' building, level 1, room 32.

I will be there in ten minutes and will give you twenty minutes only. I am a very busy person. If you do not come to me, I will ensure that you are judged for the wrongdoing that you have been a part of.

Ms Mara Hutchings

PA to Harland Barret, Premier

'She wants you to go to her,' Luca said. 'It will be a trap.'

'I have no intention of seeing her,' Kelsee replied. 'As soon as the power comes on, everyone will know the truth, Outside and Campion will come in and she will have to hide.'

'A great deal can happen in half an hour,' Alec cautioned. 'Seth warned us that even Tropolis is in danger. She had all the power over the people and now, who knows what is happening on the streets?'

'The Tropolite people will be thinking clearly, just like Kelsee,' Eban said frowning.

'Wrong!' Alec said. 'Kelsee knows what is going on, they don't.'

'I won't put them back under her command,' Eban said confidently.

Alec rubbed his forehead. 'Then we have no choice, we have to stop her. If she has no power over the people, she is likely to take it back at whatever cost.'

'Could we just get the power on and let Tropolis see the message?' asked Mercy.

Alec shook his head. 'There is no time for that, she could strike at any moment.'

'If she goes to level one, she'll see that message,' Kelsee said. 'Shut it down!'

Eban shook his head. 'There would be no point, she'll see the people.'

Luca thought about Hutchings' warning to Kelsee's safety if she did not meet her. Hutchings was trying to be intimidating, but perhaps she was worried about the evidence that Kelsee had claimed she had.

Luca wondered more about the things that Seth had warned. Hutchings was planning something much bigger than just destroying Campion. He remembered the blue shimmer of the Emundabit sensor cube when it had been live. There had been three countdown clocks; one for Campion, one for Outside and the final one for Tropolis. There had been no place that was safe.

Luca thought about the conversation Kelsee and he had with Harland about the ark, about it being the place that was safe when everything else was *cleansed*. But there had been more that Harland had said. The committee when Harland was in power had discussed implanting explosives in the city, putting chemicals in the water and using drones to start fires. Harland may have only been involved in the early ideas stage, but the drones setting fires had already happened, it was likely that the rest would follow suit. Luca swallowed hard. Hutchings had gone further than just these whims. She had invaded the Tropolites minds, she had commanded them to circle the city; the cleansing or extinction of the unchosen Tropolites might be done without harming the wealth of the city at all. Harland had spoken of a superior group emerging from Emundabit. Hutchings was speeding towards this end.

It was beginning to make sense. Hutchings was hoping that she would just need to clean up the miniscule resulting mess when Outside and Campion came into Tropolis. They would, of course, in her mind do most of the work themselves, one against the other. She could have the power plants of Outside, she could remove the ones that weren't chosen in some mysterious glorious fight to save Tropolis and yet everyone in the ark could be saved from the violence above. Emundabit was designed so that she could rule. Her rulership would be blood stained and violently taken from the people she would claim to be hers.

She was not expecting this. Outside and Campion were united and wanted to bring the cure to the fatigue into Tropolis. This was not her dream or her plan.

Luca shivered at the thought of Hutchings' desperation and loss of power. They needed to move carefully, but there was no option for caution.

He gestured to the ceiling. 'Hutchings has the command of drones and whatever else was planned for Emundabit. If Tropolis was in danger before, I think it is in even more danger now.' Luca put his hand on Kelsee's back. 'We set the meeting place,' he said. 'Tell her we'll meet her at the ark. We'll have witnesses if we need them there.' He passed the tablet to Kelsee. 'You need to show her that you set the rules.' Luca quickly explained to Alec that the ark was a mass storage space deep in the basement of the building, a place of safety should there be an attack or attack was launched. 'It seems that only a few have been invited there.'

'It will be dangerous,' Kelsee muttered lowering the tablet to her side. 'She'll be heavily guarded.'

Luca disagreed. 'Not if she is worried that you have something on her.' Luca raised the tablet. 'And she won't be expecting us to be with you.'

Kelsee took a moment to think. She looked intently at Luca. He was frightened that all he had concluded was just his imagination. But Hutchings' rushed message revealed more than that. Hutchings had thought it urgent enough to find Kelsee, desperate enough to warn her that she wouldn't find justice and unsure enough to threaten assistance be it medical or otherwise. She wanted her transfer of power to be neat. Harland couldn't give it to her, and Kelsee wouldn't be allowed to steal it. He was certain he was correct.

After a steadying breath, Kelsee typed a short message and passed the tablet back to Eban.

'To the point,' Eban said than read it aloud. '*No, I'll meet you at the ark, I bet you didn't think I'd know about that either. There are many things that I know*.' He checked that the others were in agreement and then pressed send.

Chapter 22

The lift was swift. They had a rushed discussion whether they should approach the ark another way, but it was wiser to stay together. Luca did not want to leave Kelsee alone with Hutchings.

Alec had armed himself again, but no one else chose to pick up the rifles that Atticus and Seth had used. Luca knew that he would not be able to use such a weapon. The tasers that Major Thomas had taken from them would not kill, and even that seemed odd in his hand before. He hoped that Alec would be able to protect them should they need it. He felt guilty to be hoping the Alec would be alright with harming another person. Now, standing in the lift, going empty handed seemed a very stupid decision to have made.

The lights flashed as they sped past each floor. Luca was grateful that this part of the building still retained a power source but was saddened by the reason why it mattered. Why would the rest of Tropolis be without? Perhaps Emundabit was still running. Had Hutchings reset the extinction commencement sequence? Luca lifted the tiny cube to the edge of his pocket and glanced at it. There were no lights.

The smooth descent warred against the tumultuous anxiety Luca felt. He rolled up his sleeves and then pulled them back down again. He shifted from one foot to the other. Mercy placed a hand on his shoulder but did not say anything, no one said anything. Perhaps he wasn't the only one who was uneasy.

'Our plan?' asked Luca.

Alec stood straighter. 'Arrest her. Put her on trial. Bring justice for all the people.'

Luca snorted. It sounded simple. 'Anything more detailed?'

'Kelsee and I will step out of the lift,' Alec said calmly. 'You can hide ...' Alec pointed to the two narrow corners at the front of the lift either side of the doors. 'And come out when all is clear.'

Luca stared at the numbers, his stomach churning from the thought of it. 'Good plan,' he said knowing that this was all they had and even that wasn't certain. 'Good plan,' he repeated quietly.

There was a much longer gap between the ground floor and the basement light changing. The ark was deep under the building, safely hidden from the world above. Everyone moved to their positions. The hiding places were virtually useless for three people to stand in. Alec took Kelsee's arm as if her were reprimanding her, but he was very gentle.

The elevator slowed and then came to a halt.

A quiet swish and the doors slid open.

'Alec? Kelsee.' Mara Hutchings was waiting. Her voice was as sickly sweet as it had ever been. 'What do you want with her?' she asked Alec.

'She told me about the ark. I figured that if I delivered her to you, since you seemed to have lost her the first time, I might get a place.'

She paused. 'I'm more concerned as to why you aren't already dead.' Luca could hear the vicious disappointment in her voice. 'Atticus might not be getting his place at this rate.' Her voice was sharp and cruel. 'He won't be needing that.' She cleared her throat. 'The weapon. Really man! Take the weapon!'

The gruff acknowledgment made Luca's heart race. She had not come alone.

Luca stepped out. Hutchings was standing in the centre of the crammed space. The huge pillars holding the thick ceiling were crowded with plastic wrapped pallets. Boxes were stacked up against crates marked with zone numbers. The massive storage facility was so full that the excess goods were flowing out to the lobby area.

She was dressed in the customary white Tropolite clothes, but she had accessorised her neat tailored outfit with a deep yellow broach, belt and small handbag.

There were only two men with her. She had chosen them for their strength and perhaps not for their ability to think beyond a command. It could have been Atticus or even Seth standing guard.

Hutchings suddenly looked up. She curled her nose up and squinted at Luca. 'You?' Her eyes narrowed cruelly then she began to laugh. 'Did she hurt you?' She turned down her mouth in mock sadness. 'Poor little Outsider!'

The two men laughed with her.

Luca frowned.

'Yes, it must hurt a bit.' Hutchings pointed to Luca's stomach.

He peered down and saw the large amount of deep red blood that stained his Tropolite clothes. She thought he was injured. She thought that Kelsee had hurt him. Seth's death had covered him, and he could choose to hide behind it.

Luca wanted to play to her weakness and pretend she was right. He considered stumbling over to her and begging her for help before taking out one of her men. But Luca knew that he was not strong enough to do such a thing.

He had only one other option to take her off guard.

'This?' Luca said pointing. 'Oh, this is nothing.' He prodded it and then lifted it from his stomach. 'I'm not hurt at all. Whatever gave you that idea?'

Hutchings took a step back and glared at Kelsee. 'I don't know. Do you?'

Her eyes then darted back to the lift.

'Don't mind us!' Eban said and then began to hum. Luca glanced behind.

Mercy walked over to Kelsee and stood beside her.

'You!' Hutchings said pointing at Eban.

'Yes, that's right,' Eban said smiling and pointing to his face. 'The handsome chappy from the video.'

She turned and frowned at Mercy, trying to place her.

Kelsee caught her attention again. 'I think we should have a bit of a chat, don't you?'

'I'm not here to chat,' Hutchings retorted.

'But we are,' Kelsee said. 'I want to talk to you about Emundabit and your plans to destroy Tropolis.'

Hutchings shifted a little.

Kelsee continued. 'I also want to discuss my grandfather, Harland Barret, and why you killed him.'

A deeper voice sounded from behind her. 'I'd like to talk about that too.' Alard stepped out from behind a pile of boxes.

Luca was both shocked and elated. He glanced at Kelsee who was wide eyed and opened mouthed.

Alard had seen her reaction too. His forehead wrinkled.

'Any more of you?' Hutchings asked sarcastically. 'Disarm them all,' she commanded, pushing her guards into action.

Two Campion crew appeared either side of Alard. They flanked him with their weapons trained on on her guards. 'I don't think so.' The Campion soldiers already had their marks and were not intimidated by the larger men.

One of Hutchings' guards bent down to her. 'Is it true what they are saying, is Mr Barret dead?'

'Oh, shut up!' Hutchings commanded.

'But ma'am, if Mr Barret is hurt, what will happen with the invasion?'

Luca realised that this guard had revealed that the commands via the Tropolis chip had failed. If he was aware of the warped video, and he wasn't part of Alec's compassion prize army, he must be a Tropolite; a Tropolite free to think.

Kelsee stepped forward. 'Great question!' She smiled at the man who appeared concerned.

The guard spoke again. 'Tropolis is going to get attacked and we need a leader to help us.'

'And what am I, idiot?' Hutchings asked angrily.

Kelsee didn't allow anyone to answer Hutchings' question. 'I wonder if, perhaps, the leadership should go to Harland Barret's closest relative.' She glanced at Alard and then at Luca.

Hutchings tutted. 'Stupid suggestion!' she sneered. 'I am best suited for the role since I have been Harland's right-hand *man* for all these years.'

'And yet, you are being ... what was it ... invaded?' Kelsee asked.

The guard nodded.

'You fool!' Hutchings hissed. 'We are in the ark. Nothing can happen to us.' She peered at the man and spotted his lack of conviction. 'Your family is here. What does it matter about those out there?' She recomposed herself. 'There is no evidence supporting the death of our leader.'

The second guard joined. 'He's not in the ark.'

'How little you know and understand,' Hutchings cooed. 'In the event of Barret being incapacitated, the leadership role goes directly to me.' Hutchings sighed. 'It is all in writing and completely authorised.'

Luca shook his head. 'I'm not sure the people of Tropolis would vote you in,' he said, then added with a hint of sarcasm, 'ma'am.'

Hutchings scowled. 'Of course they would,' she said to the guards, 'but that is not your problem,' Hutchings continued. 'By law I am the ruling authority.'

'Maybe a woman is no good for Tropolis at this time when we are about to be invaded.'

Hutchings closed her mouth tightly. Luca wondered if she was battling to blurt out the truth about her ruling for several years under the guise of Harland Barret. She could never own up to her success without incriminating herself.

After a moment, Hutchings brushed down her neat clothes and had composed herself again. 'A woman can be excellent as leader.'

'Oh,' the guard said, 'I'm not sure. Wasn't it a woman before Mr Barret? Didn't she leave a huge mess for Mr Barret to sort out. I mean, I don't remember it myself but I'm sure I saw it on the Network. He has made Tropolis what it is today. A woman could never do that.'

Hutchings gritted her teeth. 'We do not live in the prehistoric age.' She balled her hands and Luca was certain that she stamped her foot. He could understand her frustration. For all he knew, she could have been the one circulating the stories of the failed leadership before Harland and undermining her own abilities by doing so. She took a deep breath and then smiled. 'Well, if you choose myself or Barret's closest relative,' Hutchings pointed sharply at Kelsee, 'You will have a female lead. And who would want a girl in charge?'

Kelsee laughed. 'I wasn't claiming to want to lead. I don't think I am ready for that.'

'Then why the argument?' Hutchings screeched.

'You think I'm my grandfather's closest relative. I'm not.' Kelsee shrugged.

Hutchings frowned. 'Your grandfather raised you. I know that full well.'

'Yes,' Alard said, his deep voice strong in the crowded room. 'But I am her father and the son of Harland Barret.'

Luca staggered back a step. He looked at Kelsee and she was smiling at Alard. She wasn't shocked, she already knew. Mercy had placed her hand in Kelsee's and was nodding. Eban gave Luca his lopsided smile. All this time Alard must have known about who Kelsee was.

'You being who?' asked Hutchings. 'Our dear Harland lost his sons many years ago. Everyone knows that.'

'Lost? Or abscond?' Alard stood tall. 'I took my chance and left this regime as soon as I was able to after my brother died. My wife refused to join me in my mission.'

Alard walked around her and stood with Kelsee. She reached over to him and pulled him close. She hugged his arm.

'Brigadier Alard,' he paused. 'Alard Barret that is, of Campion. Leader of the free people of Tropolis.'

Luca supressed a gasp. They had been using his first name all this time. It made perfect sense that Alard had dropped Barret since its association was with the assumed enemy.

Hutchings laughed. 'Leader of Campion? The ones invading us! I don't care who you are, you will not take power from me.' She scowled. 'You are in my building and I can have all of you taken away.'

'But you won't,' Eban said, 'Because we have something that you want.'

'What could I ever want from you?' Hutchings said peering down her nose.

'You want the evidence to disappear,' Luca suggested.

'Taking you away and making you disappear should deal with that.'

Eban shrugged. 'But then you won't know how to stop it going out over the Network.'

'Harland hasn't been seen in person in years,' Luca said to the guards before turning to Hutchings. 'I saw him die, and you know it was your doing.'

'Ma'am?' the second guard said. 'This doesn't look like you are in control.'

'Shut up you fool. Enough.' Hutchings said reaching casually into her bag. It was over in flash and two almost silent shots. Both of her guards fell to the ground.

Luca yelped and dashed to stand in front of Kelsee.

'They were ever so tiresome, and as you can see, I'm capable of looking after myself.' Hutchings blinked slowly. 'Now, you wanted to talk about something. Evidence was it?'

Alec cleared his throat. 'I think you wanted to talk about how to get hold of the evidence.'

'And you want what in return?' Hutchings gestured to the long passage of towering parcels. 'A place in the ark perhaps.' She smiled a little too sweetly. 'If you tell me how to erase the said evidence, you would be very welcome to join me. There would be a space for you in my council.'

It unnerved Luca that Mara Hutchings could change so dramatically. She had just killed two men for being tiresome and now she was alluding to being generous. Luca knew that Hutchings would never let them in and he had no intention to trust her.

'It would be wise to hand yourself over to us,' Alard encouraged. 'I don't think the evidence is going to magically disappear.'

'Hmm.' Hutchings narrowed her eyes. 'You seem to forget that I am the power of Tropolis. I will destroy the Network and nothing that you call evidence will ever stick to me.'

Luca turned to Eban who stood relaxed and just shook his head.

Hutchings pulled back her tailored sleeve and began to tap on the watch at her wrist. 'I will be the leader of a superior race whether you like it or not. Of course, if you refuse to tell me about this so-called evidence, you won't even have a chance to like it!'

'Superior race, I've heard that said before,' Kelsee said. 'What exactly is that?'

'That, dear girl,' Hutchings replied sweetly explaining, 'Is what is in the ark.'

Luca could almost taste the foul and rotting attitude to the people in the ark. Hutchings described them as what and not who. They were not lives she was playing with but pawns in her game for ultimate power. She did not want a free people but the adoration and unending devotion of those she had saved.

'I'll give you one last chance before I start the battle.' Hutchings laughed. 'I have power that you have underestimated. You Outsiders are such a waste of space, the real dregs of Tropolis and as for Campion the *free people*,' she quoted, 'they will never rise. I have an army who will do as I say and will only listen to me. I can have them destroy everyone you care about. They hear my voice and obey my commands.'

'Is that how you intend to continue?' Alard asked. 'Do you want your so called superior ones to obey and worship you? Are you going to trap them in darkness?'

Hutchings sighed and pouted. 'Such poetry!' she declared with heavy sarcasm. 'People need to be told what to do. They are so weak and useless otherwise.'

'Useless?' Mercy asked. 'People were never meant to be just machines that obey. They were made to think and make choices. People have to find freedom. You have no right to command them.'

'But I do!' Hutchings replied smiling widely and showing her perfect teeth. 'They are far too easy to manipulate. They are already mine; they always have been.'

Luca tilted his head to one side. 'What about them?' he asked pointing the lifeless guards. 'Were they under your command?'

Hutchings peered at the bodies slumped at her feet. 'Not anymore!'

'But they weren't, were they?' Luca said. 'They questioned you, they didn't trust you, they were under your command.' Luca stepped aside so the Hutchings could see Kelsee clearly. 'And she was supposed to kill me, wasn't she? That was your command.'

Hutchings shrugged. 'I also commanded her here,' she said in defence.

'I chose to come here,' Kelsee said. 'And I chose not to obey your voice.'

'You my dear girl,' Hutchings said sweetly, 'Are a little bit unusual then.'

'Not anymore,' Eban said. 'Those men were free and so is every other Tropolite.'

Hutchings urgently tapped the watch at her wrist. She unclipped it and used both thumbs on the tiny screen. 'What have you done?'

'Let's just say, I've shed a little bit of light in that darkness.' Eban punched the air.

Luca stepped towards her. 'What will happen when the people won't choose you?'

Hutchings looked up from her tiny control panel. 'You haven't won this. They will choose me.'

'Even the ones out there?' asked Kelsee.

'They'll respond to fear if I can't command them.' Hutchings returned to the watch. 'They'll attack the Outsiders and Campion; instead of a shield, they will fight anyone trying to get in. Then I can just get rid of them. No one will know. I'll still be the hero to the ark dwellers.' Hutchings smiled but it was brief. 'You see, I have covered all the routes.'

Eban pointed to the watch. 'You may want to check what is currently playing on the Network before you claim hero status.'

Hutchings panicked as she tapped a couple more times. She paused for a moment.

Luca could see the change in her demeanour. All her extravagant planning would be based on the fact that she was safe in the ark with her people, her chosen superior race. But what would happen if all that was lost because of a rescue plan set in place by another?

She slowly looked up. Her eyes were wild and her face was fixed and angry. 'I'll kill the whole lot now.'

Luca's heart raced.

'Er,' Eban interrupted. 'How? We saw the plans for Emundabit. We knew what you planned. You couldn't attack Outside, Campion or Tropolite even if you wanted to.' Eban looked seriously at her. 'I've disabled the drones, the chemical weapons and explosives. Do you really think we'd arrange to meet you if we thought you could still carry it out?'

Hutchings frantically tapped the screen and grimaced. She looked up a smiled bitterly. 'The biggest problem has to be the human weakness of stupidity and ignorance.'

Luca exhaled, saddened by Hutchings' immovable attitude. Ignorance was not something that the powers of Tropolis had guarded against. It had been instrumental in cultivating and enhancing that culture. 'I suggest that you give yourself up,' Luca said, confident that there was nothing else that she could do.

Hutchings shook the watch and something broke off from it. She lowered it to her side.

'What will you do with me?'

Alard replied quietly and calmly. 'A trial, and I expect a prison sentence.'

'I have the best legal team,' Hutchings announced, grasping at everything that was slipping out of reach.

'We have evidence,' Kelsee said. 'It was in my grandfather's safe.'

Major Thomas had been very interested in the folder that she had taken from them. Luca knew that she was prone to be harsh but believed that she would be thorough in her investigation of the facts.

Luca spoke gently. 'You could never have ruled with a people dependant on you who couldn't think for themselves.'

'Tropolis needs a new and advanced start. All I wanted was to reset it all.'

'You can't reset the human race,' Alard said.

'We can try. Join me,' Hutchings coerced. 'I will control it all. There will be no room for failure.'

'Failure?' Luca asked. 'People being able to think for themselves isn't failure.' He shook his head. 'Why would we want to join you?' he asked with a slight sneer. Hutchings showed no remorse or regret for what she wanted to do. She was still willing to follow through in destroying everything and everyone. 'You have treated people as objects and this world as the winnings of the Prize. You can't do that. You've always been on the losing side. You could never have won this. You will be tried.'

'Your version of a trial doesn't appeal to me.'

'It will be fair,' Mercy said.

'Fair?' Hutchings scowled. 'Exactly. I don't want that level of punishment. I'm taking the last bit of power I have.'

For a moment Mara Hutchings stood silent and still. No emotion played over her face and she was all the less human for it. She swiped the watch. 'This is not what I had planned,' she finally said. She raised her hand to her mouth and swallowed. 'If I can't have it, no one will. Death to Tropolis!' she shouted before she collapsed to the floor. A glass vial rolled out from her fingertips.

Chapter 23

Mercy rushed forwards, fell to her knees and lifted Hutchings head. 'She's still breathing!'

'Medical supplies,' Kelsee instructed. 'In the ark.'

Hutchings eyes flickered open. 'No antidote to this fine poison. I've won.' She took a rasping breath. 'My world would have been better than this one.' She closed her eyes, her body slumped, and she died.

Mercy laid her down gently. 'She'll never know.'

'What a coward!' Alard accused. 'She should pay for the mess she has caused.'

'She's just lost her life,' Mercy said with tears in her eyes. 'Don't you think that is payment enough?'

Alard tutted and shook his head.

'People have suffered because of her!' Kelsee said jumping to his defence.

'We've not seen the justice we wanted,' Eban replied.

'She stole it!' Kelsee said angrily.

Eban took the watch from Hutchings grasp. He pressed her finger to the screen and the watch lit up. He gasped.

Vibrations shook the ground. A couple of the boxes tumbled from the stacks.

Eban had placed both tablets on the ground and was frantically rearranging and flicking between them and the watch.

A second rumble and the floor trembled again. Alard pulled Kelsee closer to a pillar and beckoned the others to follow. The lights flickered but stayed on.

Kelsee yelped. 'What's happening?'

'She had an exit plan,' Eban said. 'Disabling it now!' He looked up. His face was ashen. 'We need to get out of here!'

Luca noticed a dim light had flickered on at the far end of the long corridor that was made from the piled-up hoardings. Screaming and shouting preceded a small group of people who were running toward them. Their faces and clothes were blood stained and grey with dust. They were pushing and shoving each other to get away from the massive warehouse that had been organised with all that the ark needed to survive. A dark cloud of smoke billowed out from the thick concrete entrance as they ran from it.

The Tropolites took no notice of anyone else but themselves. The ones that had reached the controls first hammered the button to call the waiting lift. The door opened lazily, despite the crushing crowd that was now pushing to enter. They squeezed into the tiny box, the doors closed, and the noise was suddenly gone.

A few more from the ark arrived and punched the lift button impatiently. There were angry exchanges as they jostled to the front.

'You need to get out of here,' Alard said. 'Get to safety, whatever that might be.'

Kelsee gripped his hand. 'I've only just found you, papa.'

Alard's expression softened.

'You should have told me before,' Kelsee said frowning.

Alard bowed his head. 'I ... I ...' he stuttered, 'I didn't know how to. There wasn't any time.' He pointed to the stair well. 'I'll find you.' Alard looked hopefully at Alec.

'I'll get them out of here,' Alec said nodding.

Alard stepped into his military mode. He ordered the men with him to go into the ark and collect the people that they could find there. 'I'll be with you soon.'

'You can't!' Luca said grabbing the sleeves of the men. 'You have to leave with us.'

Alard took a step towards the dark smoke. 'There might be others.'

'There isn't time,' Eban said holding the door open to the stairs. 'Those people have escaped, but no one else will. Hutchings made sure of that.' He reached out to them. 'Hurry!'

Alard took a step towards the warehouse. There was a sudden roar.

Kelsee put her arms around him. It took a moment for Alard to respond.

'Brigadier!' Eban shouted. 'Get these people to safety!'

Alard suddenly stood upright as if jolted into realisation that there would be no survivors in this ark and responded to the command. He ushered everyone to the stairs including those from the ark.

The bright orange wall of flames licked at the concrete entrance and caught instantly on the ready-made fuel that filled the space. Everyone sped through the doorway and Alard forced the door shut behind him, just in time, as the flames poured over the small inspection window.

Luca kept running. He followed Alec and Mercy with Eban, Kelsee. Alard and his men were at the rear of the group doing their best to get the stranded Tropolites to move faster.

The flights of stairs twisted between landings. After a few floors had been climbed the air began to shimmer with dust. There was no time for discussion.

The building shook violently and a terrrifed scream bled through the wall. Luca know that the stair case was built next to the lift and he went cold. A sudden bang vibrated through the stairs and the grind and screech of the lift falling down the shaft made Luca vomit.

He wiped his mouth on the back of his sleeve and ran all the harder, desperate to get away from the death trap that Hutchings had set.

The further that they went the heavier the dust seemed. When they finally reached an exit door the air was thick and grey.

Luca's exhausted muscles carried him up the final flight of stairs and the door of the lobby. There was no time to rest or catch their breath.

'What has she done?' Alec asked.

Luca had thought that he had escaped Hutchings last stand, but she had not settled with just the ark. He tried to prepare himself for what she could have done but his mind bubbled over with numerous atrocities.

They covered their noses and mouths with whatever they could and opened the door.

The Tropolites they had escorted from the ruined ark scurried across to an exit and disappeared without thanks.

The air in the lower lobby was dense with dust and shards from the shattered windows had smashed over the floor. Sprinklers had been activated and water rained down from the ceiling causing the floor to be a dangerous mixture of broken glass and slippery mud.

Eban had Hutchings' watch and was checking the tiny screen. He wiped the tablet against his leg and then began swipe and tap on the screen.

'I disabled it before it all happened,' he said. He had tears in his eyes. 'But I was just too late. I'm sorry.'

Alard pushed them out of the panels where the windows had once stood tall and drew them back from the building. The ground was littered with layers of glass and chunks of concrete

Luca peered up at the contestants' building towering into the night sky. It no longer shimmered the unusual colour. The clean appearance was shattered as blinds and other items dangled from the blown-out windows. Water dripped from the floors above and the occasional blue spark showed that the electricity was exposed in places and was still flowing through the building.

Luca turned his attention to the space that had been guarded. He searched quickly for any Tropolites but there were none.

He put his arm around Eban. 'We're not hurt,' he said with a smile. 'You have done an incredible job.' He pointed to the empty area in front of the building. 'You helped them think clearly again and they got away.'

Eban half laughed.

They waited.

The silence was reassuring.

'She knew she had lost yet wasn't going to go alone,' Luca whispered. 'She couldn't even give that to the people she had claimed.'

Mercy wiped her face with her sleeve. 'Mara Hutchings genuinely didn't care for anyone but herself.'

Luca was stunned by Mercy's strong words but knew them to be true. He looked at Eban.

'I don't know what her full last plan was,' Eban said, 'But it was her last plan.'

A massive bang sounded from the contestants' building and Luca ducked to the ground.

'Run!' Alard shouted and gave a wide sweeping gesture to the buildings at the edges.

There was no need for any further encouragement. Everyone ran across the open space and towards the shadows of the surrounding structures. The ground shook violently, the pavement buckled and there was deafening growl from the building behind them. Luca dared to peek over his shoulder. The building was being sucked into a massive hole. It looked as if it were falling to its knees as it collapsed vertically. Huge boulder-sized chunks of broken concrete and twisted steel sections exploded out of the building. The mass of dust churned into stifling cloud. Luca ran as fast as he could.

Something hit the back of his leg hard, and his foot twisted underneath him. He lost his balance and found himself suddenly sprawled on the pavement. The crescendo of the falling skyscraper was still building and Luca dared to glance at the devastation behind him. Forgetting his own pain, he clambered upright and sped as fast as could away from the danger and towards the others.

The darkness was suddenly lit with a thousand lights shining from the apartments and buildings on the Tropolite skyline.

Eban had sprinted to the nearest light, pushed open the glass door and everyone dashed inside. He leaned out and pulled Luca inside.

The cloud of debris and dust pattered on the pane like heavy rain.

They gathered at the door watching as the view became completely veiled by the destruction of the tower.

'We need help. Tropolis needs help.' Alec put his hand on Luca's shoulder. Luca winced at the sudden extra pressure. 'It's time to bring the Outsiders and Campion in.'

Luca shrugged and shuffled away. 'It won't be safe.' He bent low to examine his leg. He was badly bruised and his ankle smarted, but other than that was seemingly unscathed. 'The Tropolites think we are going to attack.'

'Then we go to them until all this settles down,' Alec said.

Luca knew that they would have to wait before they could even leave this building and then pick their way back to the bay. He looked at his uncle with affection. Alec was ready to be reunited with his sister, Willow.

Luca looked away and back to the dust that obscured the view. He wondered if Hutchings had attacked anywhere else. Eban had said that he had stopped the Emundabit designed attacks, but they had never once thought that Hutchings would destroy her own safety. Luca considered the woman for a moment. She had been prepared for every other outcome to step into power;

perhaps this was her alternate plan if everything else failed. However, it seemed unlikely that she would even consider failing.

Luca became aware of the sound of sobbing. Kelsee was sat at an open door. An older woman was hunched on the ground trembling.

'You're safe. Everything will be alright,' Kelsee said over and over.

'We are going to die!'

'No!' Kelsee said. 'Look at me!'

The woman slowly raised her head and stared wide eyed at Kelsee. 'It is over now.'

'Kelsee Barret?' The woman shouted and then hugged Kelsee.

Other doors began to open and other Tropolites peered out into the hallway.

'It's Kelsee Barret!' she announced. She gazed in wonder at Kelsee. 'Is Harland making everything safe?'

Kelsee smiled sadly. 'Not exactly.' She paused. 'Harland Barret died quite some time ago, but I know the people who are going to make us all safe.'

'Dead? How will we be safe without him?' the woman asked then reached out and patted Kelsee on the arm. 'Dear child!' the woman sobbed again. 'You may not have any family, but you will not be alone.'

Kelsee smiled sweetly at her. 'I'm not alone.' She looked up at her friends.

The woman noticed the others stood around. All their clothes were grey and undistinguishable whether they were Tropolite, Outsider or Campion. 'You escaped, but they will attack us now.' She looked wide eyed at the group of friends. 'Harland is dead,' she said fearfully, relaying the news with a gasp. 'We have no one to keep us all alive. How are we ever going to defend ourselves without a leader? They will come after our city and destroy us.'

'Do you trust me?' Kelsee asked in a calm and quiet voice.

The woman didn't even think before nodding.

'All the attacks are finished,' Kelsee spoke to all the Tropolites that were there. 'They have been stopped.'

'How can we be safe?' another asked. 'I know they are coming for us.'

Eban shook his head. 'Enough!' he said sitting down on the floor cross legged. 'I have the original video,' he said, 'And I am setting this straight.'

Kelsee sighed. 'There will be an important message on the Network.'

'There hasn't been anything on my screen since this morning … I think.'

'Do you remember what happened to you?' Kelsee asked. 'Do any of you know what happened to you?'

Eban passed Luca a tablet and pointed to Kelsee. The screen showed that it was recording her. Luca held it steady and listened as Kelsee brought light to the dark places in the Tropolites' minds. She spoke softly and with empathy because she truly understood the confusion that they had suffered. She explained that Harland Barret had died and yet Mara Hutchings had been directing Tropolis for years. She was able to explain their lack of memory and even help them with why they felt compelled to behave strangely. She took the time to confess to being free from the fatigue. The onlookers interjected with questions but Kelsee was able to give an answer to each and every one. Alard watched with a gentle smile and his eyes sparkled. Only when these Tropolites seemed content did Kelsee just sit and be quiet with them. Finally, she said, 'We can't keep this to ourselves. We need to let everyone know what has happened here.'

A new sound flowed out from each of the Tropolite apartments. 'Greetings from Outside!' it announced. 'I am Eban, an Outsider and Compassion Prize contestant. As you can see there are quite a few of us here.' The video was playing on every screen.

Luca raised his fist into the air. 'You've done it!' Luca leaned down and hugged Eban. 'You've really done it!'

'We are all part of this, Luca.' Eban ruffled his hair.

They stepped into the woman's neat room, leaving a trail of dirty grit with each step. They watched the Network transmit the truth, possibly for the first time in over decade.

Eban asked for the tablet in Luca's hand and then transferred that video too. As soon as the broadcast from Outside had finished, Kelsee appeared on the screen, answering the concerns and giving answers to the Tropolites.

Luca pulled the tapper from his pocket and squeezed it. 'Come in tower!'

'This is the tower, over.'

'This is Luca from the remnant that left ground level three, now at the ruins of the contestants' Building in the centre of Tropolis. Mission complete. True footage of Outsider and Campion intent to assist and care for Tropolis is now being broadcast over the Network. Contact Major Thomas at the bay. It's time to send everyone in. Outsiders and Campion will be welcomed in Tropolis.'

Luca began to laugh. He took a deep breath. This is what freedom felt like.

Epilogue

The group of fourteen and fifteen-year olds had arrived early and had waited at the entrance relatively patiently. Their teacher had waved them off enthusiastically and had taken the minibus to the pick-up point. Luca had watched from the cabin until the set time, before putting on his bright jacket and attaching his radio. He opened the door to let Kelsee step through. She smiled wildly increasing the joyful wrinkles that were beginning to form around her eyes before kissing his bearded cheek. He couldn't help but respond by pulling her back and kissing her firmly on her mouth. She laughed as she zipped up her jacket. They strolled over to the gate.

'Welcome!' Luca began. 'I am Luca.'

'Hello! I am Kelsee and we are so pleased that you will be joining us today. Follow me.'

Kelsee unlocked the gate and took the lead as the class stayed fairly close on the wide walkway. It was a long walk to the walled city, but it had been decided many years before that the journey was all part of the process. Today, the sea was calm and the sun shone brightly in the cloudless sky, but even on wilder days, people chose to walk the distance instead of climbing into a vehicle.

Kelsee stopped the group at the halfway point and talked about the wall, the history and the beginnings of Outside. There were a few questions from the students but nothing out of the ordinary.

Luca found this part of the day the most difficult and was grateful that Kelsee always took the lead. He would use the time to study the group that they were guiding. Today was no different. He would pick out the ones that might remind him of the Prize contestants either by their appearance or even their character. There would be enough of them to draw on later in the presentation. One girl, with a shock of red hair caught his attention. Perhaps it was her appearance that helped him to relate at first, but there was something else about her. She was attentive to Kelsee, but she hung back from the group and didn't interact with the others, or maybe it was that they didn't associate with her.

He had seen it before.

As they approached, the wall began to tower over them and the group became quieter in its shadow. At the end of the road, a single barred external light sat over a pair of wide, solid doors that could allow a vehicle to go through the wall.

'This is Outside. Of course, this is an entry point that would have been for those that worked here. The majority of people that lived here did so without ever being given the chance to leave.'

Luca offered up the access card to the scanner as Kelsee came to the end of her section on the approach. The doors shifted slowly inwards and the smell of waste wafted through the opening.

The smell of rubbish would always remind him of his final glean and what led him away from Outside. It had been a double glean; a notebook embellished with the Campion flower and filled with the details of those that had escaped Tropolis and a small can ringpull.

He lowered his card and pocketed it. With nothing in his hands, he fiddled with the metal band on his finger. The band he wore was of greater worth than either of the gleaned items, yet without that chance find he may never have stood this side of these doors. The band had more value because of his final glean. He looked unashamedly at his wife and was grateful for all that he had to have journeyed to have found her.

Everyone but Luca, Kelsee and the girl either commented, complained or covered their noses at the stench.

'This way,' Kelsee continued, ignoring their disgust.

She led the group through the Tropolite controlled areas at the entrance. There were a few solid buildings for vehicle maintenance and staff quarters. A new space had been built for a museum, but it had remained mostly unchanged. Kelsee took the group to the right and to the platform where they could see where the barges would enter. She talked about the usefulness of recycling and renewable energy. Taking the group closer, Kelsee stopped next to a wide screen and below a security camera.

'The video that was filmed in this place was the one that changed history for all of Tropolis. Without this video, Tropolites would have never have received the cure for the fatigue and they would have undoubtedly still been suffering to this day.'

She tapped the screen and a younger Eban than now appeared. 'Greetings from Outside!' Luca smiled at his friend. He had not changed much over the years. His love for technology and communication systems had been put to excellent use. He had been employed in overhauling the Network and working with the liaison teams.

The girl with the red hair watched the video intently. It was a very familiar piece and would have been shown to this group many times over the years no doubt. She gazed across the dockland as the video panned across the people who had gathered to go into Tropolis. Luca visualised it too. He had not been a witness to these events and had often imagined the details and emotion of the scene.

Kelsee didn't speak. In high spirits the group walked towards the large concrete entrance to the heaps.

Now it was Luca's turn.

'You live in the goodness of a story turned around, but I am here to help you to understand what it took for the people of Outside and Campion to have courage. My name is Luca, but I wasn't always known by that name. I am also Outsider number 57124.'

The girl was transfixed by Luca. He addressed the whole group, but she was particularly attentive.

Luca recited the words of the script that he knew all too well since he had been instrumental in its writing. He stood with his back to the large concrete gateway. Luca glanced up. The lights above him were a constant amber indicating the output for the incinerator and the reusable waste were at a normal level. It had been a long time since they had indicated anything different. The power producing threshold levels had been reduced since the building of the wind farms off the coast and the large stretches of land fixed with solar panels. Even the Campion water wheel designs had been modified and perfected to produce clean energy. The burning of waste was at a minimum now that resources were treated with more care, but the power the plant still produced was valued and respected.

The scanning hole had been decommissioned and the heaps were no longer places where humans gleaned an existence. Of course, there were still people who worked here, but their work was well paid. A rubbish truck trundled past and the driver sounded the horn.

The group waved and laughed, their cries mingling with the seagulls that frequented the heaps of Outside.

Luca smiled. It was a privilege to come back, to be reminded and to teach the next generation.

Luca had been involved in the education of Tropolis since the fall of Mara Hutchings and the rise of the new government under Alard Barret. The whole of the voting public, not just the subjects of Tropolis, had been numbered and counted. It seemed that Alard was familiar enough with all groups; Campion, Outsiders and Tropolites. He had taken his role seriously over the past decade and had put in place many excellent and inclusive boundaries for the people as a whole to live by. It hadn't been easy. There had been resistance to some of his more Campion based ideas and he had been forced to take small steps in order for the larger advancements to be made. The whole of Tropolis was a different community filled with people who related, worked and contributed to the whole.

'As an Outsider I had no choice but to come here every day.' Luca rolled up his sleeve and pointed to his wrist where a small lump sat under the skin. 'My chip would allow me to enter the heaps, the place where the rubbish was brought from Tropolis.' He placed his arm into the round chip reading hole. 'My chip was turned off many years ago.' Luca indicated to the rubbish beyond. 'This whole area was open with refuse, much more than you see today. It would be poured out for Outsiders to glean. I would glean here daily. I had to find items that might be worth something to trade for credits; paper, metal. I would also glean food from this place so that my father and I could eat.'

Luca looked at the crowd who were still repulsed by the smell. 'This was my dinner table and my lifeline. To you it smells; to me it was my life.'

Slowly the young people began to breathe in the air without the signs of replusion. It didn't smell any different, in fact, here it was probably the strongest, but they were beginning to show some respect.

'Tropolis held the Outsiders in their city with the huge wall and the desperation of poverty. They hid us away and had no need to think or care for us.'

Luca took the group through a section of the shanty homes that had been preserved. They were given time to explore the living conditions before moving on. Of course, the metal containers were the safer and more luxurious of properties reserved for the important Outsiders. There had been a great debate as to what to do with the land that the rest of the city had been built on, but it had been wise to leave it bare once stripped. There had been a few Outsiders who did not want to be relocated and that had been a struggle to allow for their wishes to stay. Luca reminded the students of the video and the mismatched homes that had spread over the entire area. He wanted them to see it as he had seen it.

Finally, the group stood at the foot of the Compassion Gate.

'I received a scarlet envelope inviting me to the Compassion Prize. To us it was a competition that allowed a couple of Outsiders to live in the freedom of Tropolis. When your lot in life had been scavenging for food on the heaps, this was the chance for everything good to come true.' Luca explained about the tasks and the competition. He even persuaded a few of the group to take part in mock tests. When they had finished Luca lowered his voice.

'We are going to take the same journey as a Prize contestant. Imagine being an Outsider who came from this place with this smell and this life and stepping into the richness of Tropolis.'

For the first time the students were silent. Luca scanned his card and the Compassion Gate opened without a sound. They avoided the lifts and descended to the station where a Maglev waited for them.

Once aboard the warm carriages Kelsee and Luca allowed the students to ask questions again. This time, they were intelligent and thoughtful. One brave young man suggested that if he were an Outsider, he would not have helped the people in Tropolis at all. His honesty was met with several students agreeing with him.

Luca laughed. 'I would have felt the same. The Prize was the beginning of my journey. I found out who I was and what I was capable of doing. I discovered that Tropolis was far from what I had imagined. It was sick, it was desperate for help and it couldn't mend itself even with its technologies and research. Tropolis had forgotten a long time ago that people needed to be people. That they needed to have their hearts exposed to difficulties and to grow in strength because of them.' He smiled at Kelsee. 'It took a great deal of courage for Outsiders to go into Tropolis and a place that appeared to hate them and humility for Tropolites to accept help from those it had rejected.'

After a while the group began to chat amongst themselves.

The red-haired girl approached Luca.

'Excuse me,' she said.

'What can I help with?' Luca asked.

'I don't mean to be rude, but why do you do this, why do you go back to that horrid place?'

Luca ran his fingers through his hair. 'Difficult things happen to us; sometimes it is our fault and other times it is forced upon us. Outside is part of my history.'

'But is such an ugly history!'

Luca smiled and raised his eyebrows. 'I suppose.'

'You suppose?' she questioned. 'People were held captive inside that place. They weren't even treated like humans and then they go to the ones that had caused all the problems to offer themselves again.'

Kelsee nodded. 'Tropolis was trapped too. It just didn't have walls like Outside.'

The girl shook her head.

Luca opened his hands and showed the girl his chip. 'I could have had this removed, it was an offer to all Outsiders. But I chose to keep it, as did many others.' He frowned a little. 'When you live through something that is ugly and difficult it changes you, it scars you. Does that make sense?'

She nodded and listened closely.

'You see, when you have scars you can either hide them away so that others don't see them ... and ultimately don't see you ... or you can dictate what those scars represent. My scars, my chip, my number, and my name tell my story. I am who I am because I got burnt with true compassion and the scars have shaped who I am today. I go back because I can't let this world made up of imperfect people forget who they really are.'

The girl looked sad. 'I didn't want to be who I really am.' She said hastily wiping a tear from her cheek.

'Who are you?' Luca asked.

'An Outsider.'

Luca frowned.

'Both my parents are Outsiders, they live in Tropolis but never ever give up on being Outsiders.' She looked up and smiled a little. 'Thank you for helping me. I never thought I'd be proud about who I am and who they are.' She leaned closer to Kelsee. 'I never really understood my story until now.'

The Maglev stopped smoothly on a much shorter journey than it used to at a replica station. The doors raised. The station glittered with light from the mirrored mosaic ceiling. The students piled out to the platform ahead of them. Luca and Kelsee followed.

Luca grabbed his chest in surprise when he saw their teacher standing under the archway.

Mercy was as multicoloured as she had always been, only now she wore it on the outside as well as the inside.

Kelsee ran forward and hugged her friend. She reached for Luca and dragged him there too.

Luca peered at the sign over the archway which read

WELCOME TO TROPOLIS

Never was a truer word spoken.

The Compassion Fire

With thanks to ...

The Compassion Series would never have made it into print without a number of people who have helped and got behind me along the way.

Bob, you have let me be creative and released me to be who I am called to be. That is a huge gift and I am so grateful for you.

A special thanks goes to Andy Back. You're an absolute legend. You have given me hours of time and countless grammar lessons. You haven't let me get away with throw away clichés, but have pushed me to write in an engaging way. My books are better because of your 'rude' comments! You are a massive source of wisdom and encouragement.

Thanks to Pippa, Asher and Indy who made observations, spotted the typos and gave me the inspiration to finish the series. If you, as the reader, have found any mistakes, please be kind ... perhaps they were enjoying the story too much!

The spectacular covers were put together by Benjamin. His ideas were better than mine and I'm glad for them and him.

For you, the reader of my books. If you have got to this book, you must have enjoyed them ... Thank you for diving into Luca's world. Thank you for your lovely messages, kind words and for asking about the next instalment.

Lastly, I am thankful for the company of my furry, four-footed friend and writing companion. Our daily walks have given me the opportunity to look away from the screen. In those moments, I remember who I am, where my value lies, and that there is something and someone much bigger than this.

Other books in the Compassion series ...

Book 1

The Compassion Prize

WHAT IF COMPASSION WAS NOT AN EMOTION THAT EVOKED A RESPONSE, BUT WAS A PRIZE TO BE WON?

Luca leaves the poverty of Outside and enters affluent Tropolis in the hope of winning the Compassion Prize. With the help of friends Mercy and Eban, he discovers that true compassion cannot be won.

Book 2

The Compassion Gift

WHAT IF YOU DIDN'T MAKE THE GOOD CHOICE, BUT MADE THE RIGHT CHOICE INSTEAD?

Luca has been found by Campion, but he begins to feel he has exchanged one prison for another. He must do what others have only chosen to ignore. He may be free from Tropolis, but Outside is not. The clock is ticking.

Other books by Katy Hollway ...

The Times of Kerim

Bruja hunts her, hungry for power. Japh waits for her, trusting in a promise. The Remnant plans for her. And I guide, watching as the storm begins.

Kerim is tired of running. She has escaped. Her wounded hands ache and her weary body needs rest. She hides in the shadow of a strangely familiar rock crevice. Japh has been waiting years to find her, but is he prepared for the perilous events that will unfold at her discovery?

Is she ready to listen to me, her messenger? Is she ready to step into her destiny?

Kerim discovers that mankind is not all the same. That some are called to be saved.

The Days of Eliora

Si dominates her, eager for respect Caleb notices her, detecting someone unique The Remnant shuns her And I watch over, as turmoil encompasses the land Eliora lives between worlds. Disowned by one and mistrusted by the other; she has no identity. Finding solace in conflicting friendships will shape her future beyond recognition. Caleb brings relief to her testing days, but can he bring startling revelation about who she really belongs to. Will she still her confusion and listen to my message? Is her heart prepared for the battle?

Eliora does not fit. Neither the palace nor the settlement offers her a place to be who she is called to be. Join Eliora as she discovers her calling amid the slavery of her people and the tyrannical Pharaoh. Discover the unfolding story through both the human and supernatural realm.